W9-BLN-357

JADE DRAGONS

By Florence Wightman Rowland

Cover illustration by Larissa Sharina
Inside illustrations by Douglas Gorsline
Cover design by Elle Staples
© 2018 Jenny Phillips
goodandbeautiful.com
First Published in 1954

To my mother,
Mrs. John W. Eberle

Table of Contents

Chapter 1:
Wong Ting's Secret Wish

Wong Ting lay on his sleeping mat half awake, half dreaming while the little sampan rocked gently on the morning tide. The rise and fall of the boat home was as soothing as the voice of the Old One, his grandfather, who lived with them. The quiet slap of the Wu River against its wooden sides reminded Wong Ting of the lullabies his mother hummed when she put the Last Born to bed.

Sleepily Wong Ting looked up at the curved bamboo-matted roof, watching the first streaks of dawn slowly light up the small sleeping cabin. Neither the Old One, big brother Lim Sang, nor his parents were awake. Only the Last Born fretted in his corner.

Wong Ting hoped the baby would not cry out, at least not yet. This was Wong Ting's favorite time of day. It was now that he thought about the things he would buy for his family when he had as many coppers as he had fingers and toes.

But there was no time to earn extra coins. A river boy was busy from long before the first rice until the hour of full darkness. When Wong Ting was not helping to pole the small boat upriver, he was guiding the bamboo steering oar from the stern while the heavy fishing net dragged in the water, ready to catch a carp or a stickleback.

Wong Ting rolled over, pillowing his head on his arms. It was fun to dream and plan. For the Old One, Wong Ting would buy a length of cloth large enough for a padded robe, because

Grandfather shivered in the damp night air. The one gown he owned was as thin with age as the man who wore it.

Wong Ting did not have to think twice about what Father wanted. Most of all he wanted a new, strong net that would not break, not even against the lunge of a swift, sharp-nosed river wolf, or from the great weight of a flatfish. But more than a net, Father needed new trousers. Each time they tore, Mother scolded noisily, "The cloth is too worn to hold thread, my husband." But she always managed somehow to mend them once more.

As for Mother, Wong Ting knew what she wanted. He had never heard her complain at the slowness of earthenware to boil water, but many times he had seen her quiet look of longing whenever a metal merchant poled his raft past them on his way to a market jetty. The platform of logs was always piled high with copper kettles.

Wong Ting could picture in his mind Mother's happy smile as it would be mirrored upon the reddish brown metal. He often imagined one of those fat, rounded kettles sitting proudly above their charcoal fire, singing merrily as the water changed into steam.

For the Last Born, Wong Ting would get some sweets. His baby brother had tasted nothing but rice with fish or vegetables in it, and, once or twice, bean curd with green garlic. Wong Ting smiled to himself as he thought about the funny faces the Last Born would make at his first taste of a sugar lump.

Wong Ting flipped over on his back. It was plain to him what his big brother wanted. Wong Ting often caught Lim Sang smiling across the water at the dark-eyed girl in an orange-colored sampan. She was the eldest sister of Tsu Li, Wong Ting's best friend.

Of course Mother knew about Lim Sang and the dark-eyed girl. Mother had often promised, "When the money belt sags with heaviness, we will buy a much larger sampan for us who are so crowded. Then Lim Sang can have this one." But, no matter how hard or how long they fished, that happy day had not yet come.

In his imagination, Wong Ting saw them climbing into a much larger boat—a boat big enough to have two straw-matting sails, not just one as their present one had. Then those at the poles could rest more often when the Winds of Heaven billowed the sails, speeding them on their way.

Now Wong Ting sighed wistfully, pushing a strand of black hair out of his eyes. What of himself? What would he get for himself when he had as many coppers as he had fingers and toes? Wong Ting wanted something that money could not buy. In his heart was a secret wish. Only he knew what it was: *Wong Ting wanted to walk on the land.*

Kicking aside his covers, he pulled up the legs of his padded cotton trousers and looked down at his bare feet. He wiggled his toes, wondering what it would feel like to walk on the land. Never in his life had he felt the earth beneath him. Wong Ting had been born and reared on a boat, as Father had been, and as Father's father before him, and on and on, far back across the centuries to the first boat dwellers of China.

However, Wong Ting must be careful not to let his parents know about his secret wish. Nor Grandfather, or Lim Sang. They, like all river people, looked down upon land men, feeling sorry for those who must live in mud huts. River people were glad, too, that they did not have to gaze at the same magnolia tree every day and hear the same bird songs among the cherry blossoms.

Indeed, river people did not have to look at the same thing twice unless they wanted to. They were free to drop their anchor stone in a different place every night. Sometimes they slept in the harbor, and often they stayed in the south or north canals. Under their curved, thick bamboo-matting roof, no rain could seep through to disturb their dreams as they slept the darkness away.

River people were very blessed. All through the day there were many interesting sights on the Wu. Often large cargo rafts, floated by air-filled goatskins, skimmed by. Cheerful flower boats on their way to market brightened the river. Besides, many houseboats of various sizes and shapes could be seen, and there were quite a few clumsy junks carrying grain and salt, their wing-shaped, straw-matting sails held in place by bamboo bracings. But best of all were the swift passenger steamers which anchored in midstream where the water was deep. These could move fast—faster than a water snake.

In fact, river people could watch a different scene every moment until their eyes grew tired of looking. Even then they could not see everything there was to see upon the busy Wu and along the banks of this wide, long river, one of the many in southern China.

Wong Ting sighed again. No, he must not tell his parents that he wanted to walk on the land. Even if he chose his words with thoughtful care, explaining that he only wanted to feel the earth beneath his padded cloth shoes *just once*, they would be most unhappy. They certainly would not understand it at all. They might think he did not like to live on a sampan. Indeed, they might think he wanted to be a land man. That was not true.

Suddenly Wong Ting's thoughts shifted to his friend, Tsu Li. Wong Ting remembered what Tsu Li would say if Wong Ting were to tell his friend about this secret wish. No doubt about Tsu Li's reaction. There would be astonishment and disbelief on his round face. His words would be full of scorn when he said, "You speak as the poor madman speaks—without making sense." The pressure of Tsu Li's arm about Wong Ting's shoulders would then tighten as if to make up for the harshness of his rebuke.

Smiling to himself, Wong Ting kept on building up this

imaginative picture in his mind. The scene seemed so real to him that he could almost see a puzzled frown on Tsu Li's brow. Wong Ting could almost hear the worried tones of Tsu Li's words as he asked, "Why does my friend, who is like a brother to me, tease me with such nonsense?"

At this point Wong Ting would quickly suggest a game of kick-the-marbles, thus stopping further questions. Not even a friendship as strong as theirs could help Tsu Li to understand how Wong Ting felt about wanting to walk on the land.

But no matter how impossible this dream might be, Wong Ting kept on dreaming it, never for a moment giving up on his plan to feel the earth beneath his padded shoes just once. However, Wong Ting was wise enough not to tell his secret wish to anyone, and, most of all, not to Tsu Li.

Stretching lazily, Wong Ting turned over again and dozed a while. He was finally wakened by loud, angry tones. He sat upright, blinking sleepily.

As he listened, Father roared, "Another man's back would break under my load of troubles."

Wong Ting's heart pounded hard. What had happened? Had another sampan crashed into theirs, ripping a plank loose? Was there a gaping hole torn in the bow? He had felt no bump. Had the Last Born crawled out on deck last night and fallen overboard? Wong Ting shuddered at the thought. Still only half awake, he looked anxiously across the cabin to the far corner where the baby slept and smiled to see the tiny lump which was the Last Born under his coverings.

When Father shouted, "The Fortune of Heaven is not with us this day," Wong Ting was wide awake. Now he knew something was wrong. Very wrong! He waited no longer. Quickly, he threw off his covers and shoved his bare feet into his padded shoes. Then he stepped to the cabin door. In his haste, he forgot his round skull cap.

Wong Ting did not take time to roll up the bamboo curtain in front of the door but squeezed past it into the chilly dampness of a thick fog. He shivered in spite of the thickness of the padding in his trousers and shapeless coat. The coolness of the air made the morning feel more like a day in the winter than one in the tenth or Kindly Moon.

Father was sitting on a bench at the bow, his head in his hands. Mother was trying to comfort him, but he pushed her away. In a discouraged voice, he continued, "The money belt will indeed be empty before this day is gone."

Legs wide apart, Wong Ting kept his balance on the swaying deck, feeling the restless tide beneath his feet. His heart ached for Father. He looked so tired, so very worried.

Glancing toward the shore, Wong Ting did not see the familiar buildings of the City of Min as he had expected, although last night they had dropped their anchor stone close to the harbor. Instead, there were wide stretches of flat farm lands. Here were no curved roofed pagodas, no high walls, no narrow, winding streets full of shops and eager customers. Only rows of cabbage and bean plants could be seen. Only a few huts were clustered together near the rolling hills in the distance, probably the homes of the farmers who worked this land.

Wong Ting guessed at once what had happened. While they slept the darkness away, their sampan had somehow lost its anchor stone and drifted downstream past the south canal, clear to the City of Wang at the mouth of the river Wu. Just beyond Wang Bay splashed the mighty waves of the South China Sea.

Chapter 2:
The Frayed Rope

Wong Ting stood on the deck, a frown on his usually cheerful face. He looked anxiously from Mother to Father and back again.

Father's voice was full of despair when he said, "Half a day's fishing time will be lost."

Seldom did river people come this far downstream. Here the current was too swift and dangerous, except in the warm months of the Lotus Moon and the Moon of Hungry Ghosts. They certainly never made such a trip in this, the month of the Kindly Moon. After summer was over, the ocean waves, where the river Wu emptied into the bay of Wang, were too strong and unsafe for boats as small as sampans.

The Winds of Heaven did not blow hard during the sixth and seventh months. It was then that river people eagerly tried their fortune in the deep waters of the sea. The long journey often proved quite successful. The old water lines on the sides of their boats frequently disappeared out of sight because of the heaviness of the sea's gifts. Usually the decks were covered by large flatfish.

Once, when Wong Ting was only half as big as he was now, they had caught a sailfish that was taller than the Old One, and he was the tallest man in their family.

Indeed, there were tales told from mouth to mouth how the net of a sampan such as theirs held within it a sailfish so big those river people could not pull it into their boat, fearing it would sink. Somehow, they had managed to pole back across the choppy waters of the bay of Wang, dragging their prize behind them. With the sea breeze filling their small sail, they slowly brought this big fish upriver to a market jetty. Wong Ting wished many times that they could catch such a sailfish; then his secret dreams for them would come true and all at once.

Mother now placed a gentle hand on Father's arm. This time he did not shout. "That rope had much life in it," he went on, as if he were thinking out loud. "It should have held even against the Winds of Heaven." Shaking his head wearily, he continued, "I just can't understand it. No storm, and yet our anchor stone lies buried in the mud, lost to us forever."

"We will find another, my husband."

"That is not an easy thing to do," he replied crossly. "Last year when we needed one, Lim Sang and I searched and searched. We did not find a stone heavy enough until long after third rice. Indeed, not until full darkness closed around us, and it was the best anchor stone we ever had. Now it sleeps in the mud."

Mother smiled her gentle smile, and her voice was full of hope. "Many carp might swim into our net this day," she said in her quiet way. "Perhaps we might even catch a river wolf."

Leaning against the gunwale, Wong Ting drew in his breath sharply. A river wolf! That would be wonderful. Just one of those large fish would make Father smile again. He would soon forget about the lost anchor stone and the frayed rope if they caught a river wolf.

Father sat quietly a moment, twisting the broken end of the anchor rope between his fingers. "The Fortune of Heaven is not with us this day," he said again, shaking his head wearily from side to side.

Father was right. The Fortune of Heaven was not smiling on them this day. It was going to be a long, hard pull against the current all the way back. Besides, their straw-matting sail could not help to speed their journey. With the Winds of Heaven blowing downstream, their sail would have to stay rolled up against the bamboo cross tree, idle and useless.

Wong Ting hoped that someday they would be able to buy a real anchor, one with four prongs, like those used on junks, only smaller. The sharpened ends of the metal would then grip the mud, keeping their boat home from ever again drifting southward while they slept the darkness away.

Smiling brightly, Mother offered, "Perhaps the wind will change before long."

Father shrugged his shoulders. "Even so, Heaven does not smile on us this day. Must I not buy a new length of rope? Must we not seek another stone and pull it from its home in the mud?"

Impatiently he added, "Come! Enough of talking. Wong Ting, arouse Lim Sang. And your grandfather. The Old One will steer toward the north canal while we three work. When you tire, he will take your place."

Wong Ting squared his shoulders, drawing himself up as tall as possible. Couldn't Father see that he was almost grown up? Wasn't a boy who was eleven Lotus Moons old half a man already? Was not he taller than Father's shoulder? A determined look came into Wong Ting's black eyes. He would prove he was no longer a child. He would stay with the poling as long as Lim Sang did, or longer.

Stepping quickly into the sleeping cabin, Wong Ting saw that his brother was lying there with opened eyes, one hand tucked comfortably under his head.

"This is not time for daydreaming," Wong Ting began, and he told all about the sad happening. Then he called the Old One and stopped for a moment to play with the baby. Wong Ting finally stepped back on deck; Lim Sang was already busy with the work of poling.

The stiff breeze was still blowing straight out to sea as Wong Ting lifted a bamboo pole from the mat-covered deck. He went to the bow and started in, pushing hard against the tug of the tide and the strength of the wind.

By the time full daylight had come, Wong Ting's arms ached, and his hands were beginning to blister. He gritted his teeth and pressed his lips against each other to keep the painful gasps back.

Up and down. Up and down. Lifting and pushing. Lifting and pushing once more. It became a slow, steady rhythm, like the turning of a water wheel. Lift and push! Lift and push! The palms of Wong Ting's hands were soon raw and sore, but he did not put down the pole. He wanted to prove he was almost a man by doing the work of a man.

So intent was he on his job of poling, he did not turn when Mother came to the door of the cabin.

"The rice is tender enough, my husband, even for the toothless gums of the Old One," she announced.

Lim Sang usually ate with the men, but today Father ordered, "Stay with the poling, Lim Sang. Wong Ting needs help to hold against the current."

Without a word Mother took the steering oar, freeing the Old One from his task. The men disappeared inside the cabin.

Knowing the grueling job ahead, Wong Ting bent to the steady lifting and pushing. Doggedly he kept up with the work until Father and Grandfather finished eating.

When they stepped back on deck, Wong Ting needed no urging. His stomach had been growling from the emptiness. Dropping his pole and kicking it out of the way under the port gunwale, he went into the small roofed room. He sat down near the center bowl of steaming food—brown rice, salted turnips, and pickled cabbage. Eagerly he began to scoop out some into his smaller bowl with his chopsticks. But he dropped the slender bamboo sticks almost immediately.

Leaning toward him, Mother said, "What is this?" She grasped his hands, turned them upward, and looked at the broken blisters and the redness of the skin. "This soreness I will mend," she said kindly.

In the corner where the charcoal fire still glowed red, she found clean rags. Soon cloths soaked in bean oil were tied tightly against Wong Ting's raw palms.

"By the time the first rice is over," she promised, "the heat will be gone from your hands."

Wong Ting smiled bravely, trying to hide the stinging hurt. He went back to his food, but he had difficulty holding on to his chopsticks because of the bandages.

When he saw that Lim Sang had nearly emptied the center bowl, Wong Ting asked crossly, "Is my brother so hungry, he eats my share, too?"

"A man has need of more food than a boy," Lim Sang muttered through a mouth full of rice.

Before Wong Ting could reply to these words, Mother nodded toward the fire. "There is more keeping warm," she chided, thus stopping the quarrel before it began.

The Last Born sat on Mother's knee. She fed him from her own bowl, shoving bits of food into the small, red mouth. Once the baby snatched her chopsticks and held them tightly in a chubby, dimpled fist.

Wong Ting could not help laughing. Leaning across the center bowl, he pushed gently on the tiny fingers, but the Last Born held on until Wong Ting offered him a piece of a cork fishing float.

As the Last Born clutched at the toy, he blew a mouthful of rice down the front of his padded coat. Mother scolded softly, "Go hungry, Wasteful One." Scraping the brown kernels from his clothes, she ate them herself and put him down on his sleeping mat.

Lim Sang chewed his food quickly, and so did Wong Ting. In a short time, his brother jumped up and hurried outside to help with the poling.

As Wong Ting finished, Mother asked, "How are your hands now, my son?"

Wong Ting pulled off the rags. The fire had gone from the blisters. Smiling, he said, "They're much better." But when he saw the worried look in her black eyes, he hurried to add, "They're almost well. The sting is gone."

Walking toward the fire, she ordered, "Tie up the Last Born, Wong Ting. I will soon be too busy to watch him."

Wong Ting took the Last Born out on the deck and found the short piece of rope fastened to the center post below where the rolled-up sail was tied. He wrapped the free end about his brother's trouser leg near the small ankle, knotting it just above the cloth shoe. Then he lifted the baby to the safety of a three-legged stool, again putting the piece of fishing float in his chubby hands.

"There," Wong Ting said, smiling down at him, "now you have something to play with. Now you cannot fall into the Wu while we are busy with our work."

The Last Born listened gravely, as if he understood every word, turning the smooth chunk of cork over and over again.

As if he knew how tired Wong Ting must be, Father said, "The dip net needs mending, my son."

Wong Ting obeyed, secretly glad at this chance to rest. He pulled the small net down from the cabin roof by its long bamboo handle. Leaning against the gunwale, he braced the large bamboo circle with his feet. Its top edge came up to his chin. Carefully he fingered the tightly woven webbing, studying it for holes and weak places through which fish might find freedom. This was always a tedious chore, but especially so today because of the stiffness of his hands. He found a hole and slowly began to work.

It was important that this net be properly mended. Each time their larger net caught fish, it was Wong Ting's job to handle the dip net. It was he who scooped out the fish while the others held the heavy netting high, forming a pocket in which the fish were caught. It was not easy to lift the river's gifts to the top of the Wu. Feeling proud and excited, Wong Ting always worked as quickly as he could, dumping the wiggling mass into one of the tall bamboo baskets on the deck.

This morning as Wong Ting found the weak places in the dip net, he thought about his secret wish to walk on the land. He wondered if he would ever feel the earth beneath his padded shoes.

As he daydreamed, he watched Mother. With quick movements, she was busy filling a wooden bucket with river water to scrub the deck clean. This she did every morning unless the Rains of Heaven came. When the sun shone she also washed their clothes, hanging them over poles fastened against the cabin walls. These sturdy bamboo posts slanted back along the deck and extended a short distance out over the river. While the garments were drying, everyone who wished to get from the bow to the stern of the sampan had to duck under the low cabin roof and walk through the small sleeping room.

Wong Ting glanced to his right and suddenly noticed a wide opening on the edge of the land dividing a field of cabbage in half. "Look there, Father," he said. "I've never seen that canal before."

Father stopped his pole long enough to look across the river in the direction Wong Ting was pointing. "That is not a canal, even though it is as large as the north canal."

Lim Sang was also gazing at the wide opening in the land. "Is that the new irrigation ditch the market men told you about?"

Father nodded. "Yes. When the Rains of Heaven do not come, that big wooden gate is lifted, bringing water from the river to the thirsty plants. See the big wheel?"

"Yes, Father," Lim Sang answered. "I have never seen a stouter, larger wheel."

"It can be turned from the land side or from the river. As it turns, the gate lifts and the river rushes in, filling the ditch full of water. The farmers guide this water between the rows of cabbage, or they use it to flood their rice paddies. We need more such ditches to help through the dry spells. Such droughts come often to plague those who work the land."

The sun, which had been hiding behind some clouds all morning, now came out full and hot. Its sudden warmth made Wong Ting feel sleepy. He leaned against the gunwale, his hands idle on the dip net.

Father turned around and stopped poling while he wiped the perspiration from his brow with the sleeve of his padded coat. A look of anger crossed his face when he saw Wong Ting doing nothing. Father sounded tired and cross when he asked, "Why dawdle? Only the rich can sit with empty hands."

Wong Ting's face reddened at the rebuke. Although ashamed of his laziness, he was quick to explain, "The net, it is as good as new, my father. I am finished. Every hole has been mended, every frayed knot retied."

Without answering Father returned to the endless task of poling. Wong Ting put the dip net back on top of the cabin roof and picked up his pole.

At the next bend in the river Wu, sunlight danced brightly upon something white not far from where Wong Ting was poling. It was easy to see the size of the stone, at least the part that stuck out of the river bank. Why, he thought, that would make a fine anchor stone for us, if it is heavy enough.

Wong Ting pointed with an eager finger. "Look there," he shouted excitedly. "Is not that as big a stone as the one we lost last night?"

Lim Sang and Father shaded their eyes against the sun's

glare. Father smiled. "Your eyes are as sharp as an eagle's. Had it not been for you, the rest of us would have passed by this Gift from Heaven."

Wong Ting's heart beat a happy rhythm of gladness. Now they would not have to take good fishing hours to look for a stone. Now they would not have to toss ropes into deep water, trying to loop one around the slippery sides of a stone. This one would be easy to pull into their boat. He hoped Father would find it just right for an anchor.

Wong Ting's eyes sparkled with excitement at this good happening. The Fortune of Heaven did indeed smile on them this day, in spite of its unhappy beginning.

Soon Father was tapping his pole against the stone as if testing its weight and strength. The dull thud must have satisfied him, for he gave his approval. "It will do."

Lim Sang leaned far out of the sampan. At the very first try, he looped a rope around the Gift from Heaven. Wong Ting saw how carefully his brother and father worked. Wong Ting held his breath anxiously, afraid at any moment the stone would slip from the ropes into deep water.

No doubt about how it got up there on the high bank. During the last monsoon, the waves must have washed away the earth from around this stone, leaving it there to shine in the sunlight.

Now it was theirs because Wong Ting's eyes had seen it. Now they would not drift downstream again. With the stone to burrow in the mud wherever they chose to sleep, their sampan would stay where it was anchored.

It was long past second rice before they reached the quiet waters above the harbor of the City of Min. Many boats drifted close by, dragging nets. Each river family was intent on fishing.

Wong Ting remembered what his mother had said that very morning. "We might even catch a river wolf."

Oh, how he hoped her words would come true! If that

happened, they would all forget about the frayed rope which had caused the long, hard poling upstream and the many lost fishing hours.

Wong Ting kept watching for the orange-colored sampan. He longed to tell Tsu Li about finding the new anchor stone and how they had drifted downstream last night while they slept the darkness away. However, in spite of his eyes being as sharp as an eagle's, Wong Ting did not see his friend anywhere. Perhaps later on in the afternoon, Wong Ting would hear the familiar greeting being shouted across the Wu: "Good day and good fishing," and it would be Tsu Li calling out the words of good cheer loved by all river families.

Chapter 3:
The Traveling Box Theater

When they reached the fishing grounds far above the City of Min, Father shouted impatiently, "Ready the net!"

Everyone hurried to do his own special task. Even the Old One, who seemed too frail for such hard work, helped to pull down the pile of netting from the cabin roof. He also helped to shove back the first two sections of the curved roofing until they rested upon the third, making room on the deck for the work of the day.

Wong Ting looked anxiously at Grandfather's red face and noticed how fast the Old One was breathing. Should he be doing such heavy tasks? This worried Wong Ting. Yet if anyone dared to suggest that Grandfather sit in the sun while the others worked, he would have been most unhappy. Had not he said many times that a man was worth something if he could fish? No one would think of suggesting that nine times nine was too old to help bring in the day's catch.

With many hands to help, the net was soon lowered into the river. Its weighted edge scraped against the muddy bottom of the Wu, while the top rested on the surface of the water, held up by many cork floats. To prevent the long net from being lost, it was lashed to the gunwale in several places in the stern. The boat was poled slowly upstream, dragging the heavy net behind, and the fishing began.

As the minutes passed, Wong Ting kept hoping that Mother was right—that they would catch a river wolf this day.

About every hour Father would say, "Up with the net."

At his words everyone dropped his pole, kicking it out of the way. Even Mother stopped what she was doing to help lift an end of the heavy, water-soaked net. Each one pulled and pulled with all of his strength until the sides drew together, forming a purse-like shape. The squirming fish were held safely within this large pocket.

How excited they became! How they chatted to each other! The more fish they had, the more coppers would find their way into the money belt. Of course, many times Father bargained, not for coins, but for rice and vegetables, for sprouted beans or a bit of pork. It took much food to fill six hungry mouths.

Today, at Father's nod, Wong Ting stepped closer. Holding the long handle tightly, he slanted the wide bamboo circle of the dip net, scraping it against the sides of the purse-shaped pocket of the larger net. Hopefully, he began to raise it. There was a great heaviness within. Could it be a river wolf? Wong Ting doubted that. A river wolf would be lunging, trying to break through the webbing with its sharp, pointed nose. The fish now in the dip net hardly moved at all.

By the time Wong Ting lifted the heaviness over the gunwale, he was breathing hard with his effort. Spilling its contents into one of the tall bamboo baskets, he saw only two large carp, four or five stickleback, and a few others.

Father grunted, as if not liking the size of the catch. Almost at once he shouted the order to lower the net. After it was again in place, Wong Ting looked around the deck for the two Japanese catfish and the snake-head mullet that had not fallen into the basket. He found them behind the three-legged stool where the Last Born still sat watching them at their work while he played with the fishing float.

Why couldn't there have been a river wolf in the dip net instead of these other fish? Wong Ting's bright eyes clouded over with his disappointment.

Suddenly from across the river came a happy shout. It was Tsu Li in the orange-colored sampan. A tall, slender girl stood close to him. On the other side were his three small sisters. Wong Ting never could keep their names straight. He did not even try. In fact, he chose to tease them by calling them the giggling three. Tsu Li also plagued them with this nickname, in spite of their many protests.

Lim Sang was now waving at the dark-eyed girl. In a loud, happy voice, he called out, "Good day and good fishing."

"Good day and good fishing," she replied cheerfully, her red lips curving quickly into a smile directed at him.

Wong Ting wished Father would ask the Old One to steer closer to the orange-colored sampan. Wong Ting wanted to tell Tsu Li about finding the new anchor stone and how they had slept the darkness away as they drifted downstream. But Wong Ting knew this could not be done. There were too many other boats between theirs and the orange-colored sampan. Besides, neither family could afford to fritter away good fishing hours.

Regretfully, Wong Ting watched his friend going farther and farther away with each passing moment. All they had managed was an exchange of greetings. Soon only the tip of the tall mast could be seen. Then even that disappeared behind the wide, wing-shaped sails of a big junk.

By the time the sun had begun to move toward the distant hills in the west, Wong Ting's arms and shoulders ached with the tasks he had performed.

Now, as Wong Ting scraped the dip net against the sides of the larger net, he was glad when Father said, "That is all for this day."

Dumping out the fish, Wong Ting heard something thud against the mat-covered deck. With eager quickness, Father was beside the large lump which had fallen from the net, his sharp knife scraping away at the tangle of old roots around it. Wong Ting could not understand what made Father smile.

In a loud, pleased voice, he said, "Look what we found. An anchor chain! It has slept a long time in the mud, but it is just what we need to hold our anchor stone."

Lim Sang asked, "Did it come from a river steamer?"

"No, it is too small a link for that. More than likely a river houseboat lost it. But it is just right for us. Now we do not need to rob the money belt for a length of stout rope. This metal chain will last for years."

A great thankfulness filled Wong Ting's heart. Of course, he was disappointed that they had not caught a river wolf, but an anchor chain seemed much more important to Father.

Smiling, he said, "Steer for the market jetty, my son. I am more than satisfied."

Wong Ting walked to the steering bench, giving the Old One a chance to rest inside the cabin. As Wong Ting kept the bow pointing toward the City of Min, he hummed happily to himself. Now there was a smile on everyone's face because of the anchor stone. As the Winds of Heaven billowed the sail, they sped southward. While the sampan skimmed swiftly through the water, Mother sat on the three-legged stool, holding the Last Born in her arms. Rocking slowly back and forth, back and forth, she began a haunting lullaby. Lying against her shoulder, the baby closed his eyes and was soon asleep.

When the rooftops close to the harbor came in sight, Wong Ting stared wistfully at the curved road near the river's high bank and wondered again how it would feel to walk on the land. Looking around at his family, he saw no similar desire in their faces. Instead, he thought he saw scorn in their eyes and pity, too, for the land-bound people who must be chained to the earth.

From his place at the steering oar, Wong Ting could see chair coolies pulling rickshaws or carrying beautifully carved sedan chairs. In the distance, to the south, rose the merry tinkle of children's voices as they played in the high-walled courtyard not far away.

Crowds of people hurried by. Wong Ting wondered where they all lived and what they ate. How did they earn their coppers for rice and clothing? Certainly they did not fish. Not on the land. Wong Ting laughed out loud as he thought about that.

Father turned to look at him as if he wondered what had caused his son's sudden mirth. But he did not speak.

Just ahead of the bow was a long wooden platform built far out over the Wu. It was the market jetty where Father always traded his fish for the many things a big family needs.

Ropes were soon tied tightly to one of the stout support posts. Then almost at once the lively bargaining began. Half listening to the haggling over the price of the day's catch, Wong Ting noticed a crowd of eager children with their amahs. They were standing in front of a tiny traveling box theater. The back of the puppeteer was toward the river. But from the expressions on the happy faces turned upward to the miniature stage, the boys and girls and their nurses were delighted by the little hand puppets.

Wong Ting sighed wistfully. How he wished that he could see the playlet! He would like to see the tiny stage just once!

He stretched his neck as far as he could, not wanting to miss anything that was happening up there on the high river bank. If he watched, he might catch a glimpse of the tiny stage when the puppeteer was finished with the play.

Wong Ting was so busy watching the theater box that he did not see the bright green sedan chair until four bearers set it down to one side of the crowd very close to the edge where Wong Ting stood. Then he could not help seeing a lady's slender hand pushing aside the green silk curtain at the small window. He was close enough to see the flash of sunlight sparkle on the jewels in her wide silver bracelet.

But it was not the red rubies and the green emeralds around the edges that pleased him most. Dangling from the bracelet were three small, fat dragons, each no bigger than his smallest finger. These little jade dragons, the same color as new apple leaves in springtime, danced each time her arm moved. Wong Ting had never seen anything quite like it before. He would never forget it. Never!

The graceful white hand tossed something into the puppeteer's coin box. Wong Ting heard the tinkling sound it made as it rolled around on the metal bottom. The hand then motioned downward toward the river, toward the sampan in which Wong Ting was standing.

The box theater began turning around slowly. Supported on its four high legs, it now faced him. The puppeteer began to unfasten the black cloth curtain that was stretched across the small stage. As it dropped down, Wong Ting gasped in delight at a cluster of magnolia trees at the back of the box theater. They looked real even though they were no taller than Wong Ting's hand.

Feeling an insistent tug at his knees, Wong Ting stooped over quickly, lifting his baby brother to the gunwale so that the Last Born could also see the playlet. Wong Ting kept an arm about the small waist to steady the boy on the narrow ledge.

The others in the sampan were also watching for the appearance of the hand puppets. All except Father. He was too busy with the business of selling fish to bother about a puppet show.

What a shame Tsu Li was not here to enjoy this, too! But Tsu Li's father sold his catch at another jetty north of the city.

The puppeteer ducked down and disappeared under the black cloth behind the box theater. After he was hidden from his audience, he began to narrate the story. In a high, nasal voice, he said, "In the long, long ago, two young soldiers…"

Before Wong Ting could blink, two small hand puppets appeared on the stage, dressed in military coats and hats. As he watched, they began to march up and down the small road in front of the tiny magnolia trees.

At this moment a girl puppet, dressed in a flowing blue robe embroidered with gold, walked onto the stage. It was plain to see that the soldiers were trying to impress the lady with their fine marching and bright new uniforms.

Almost at once, as the narrator went on with the story, the two men pulled out swords and began to fight a duel. Each of them wanted the lady for his very own. The small blades moved quickly. It was exciting.

Wong Ting sighed happily, gripping the Last Born tighter because he was becoming restless. This puppet show was indeed a feast for the eyes. But it was over too soon. One soldier finally fell to the ground. The victor walked off with the beautiful lady whom he had won fairly.

Thinking that this was the end of the playlet, Wong Ting wondered why the black curtain was not pulled up over the stage. Almost at once the voice of the puppeteer spoke again. Scene two had begun.

Wong Ting missed nothing. He saw an ugly yellow tiger creep out on the stage. From the other side came the young soldier and his lady love.

The tiger must have seemed real to the Last Born. When the animal roared, the baby hid his face on Wong Ting's shoulder, whimpering. Wong Ting said gently, "It is nothing to fear. The tiger won't hurt you."

At these words the Last Born raised his head and looked up at the stage, leaning against his brother as if to find comfort by being closer to him.

Looking into the box theater, Wong Ting watched breathlessly as the tiger circled the two little puppets who were standing in the middle of the stage. As the animal crept around them, the soldier pulled out his tiny sword to protect his lady love. The shiny blade moved quickly, and the tiger lay in a heap at last.

There was no doubt about what the puppeteer was doing now. Stepping out from under the black cloth, he smiled down at his sampan audience, bowing to them. Then he reached around to pull up the curtain to hide the stage. The next moment he had lifted his box theater off the ground and started up the winding road.

The Last Born squirmed impatiently until Wong Ting sat him down on the three-legged stool. When he began to cry, Wong Ting knew what was wrong. He looked on the deck until he found the fishing float. As soon as he put the smooth chunk of cork into his brother's fingers, Wong Ting remembered his Kind Lady.

Stepping to the gunwale, Wong Ting called out in a loud, grateful voice, "Thank you! Thank you very much!"

But she could not hear him. The bright green sedan chair was gone.

Chapter 4:
The Orange-Colored Sampan

The dismal days of winter came all too quickly. Wong Ting shivered in the icy dampness of the Bitter Moon. Everyone in his family stuffed rags inside his clothing to try to keep warm, for none owned more than one padded coat.

Whenever he was not helping with the fishing, the Old One huddled under the shelter of the cabin roof. Much of the farm land on the banks of the river Wu now brightened with the green of young wheat plants.

One cool afternoon, long before the fishing time had gone, Father spoke to Wong Ting. "Steer for the market jetty. Lim Sang and I will stretch the nets to dry."

Soon their sail filled with the stiff breeze, and the little sampan skimmed lightly over the water.

As Wong Ting guided them between the many boats and rafts, Father fastened a pole to the bow, pointing it upward toward the gray clouds overhead. Lim Sang likewise fastened two lengths of bamboo to the stern, close to where Wong Ting steered. With much grunting and yanking, they managed to drape the heavy webbing across these three poles high above their heads and the cabin roof.

Skillfully, Wong Ting made his way along the crowded Wu, wondering why they were now headed for the market jetty. There was still much good fishing time left to this day. Why were they leaving in the middle of the afternoon? But Wong

Ting did not put these thoughts into words. No one questioned a father's orders. Not even a mother dared to ask why this or that was so.

The Old One sat down next to Wong Ting. This was a chance that could not be missed. Seldom did they have time for just talking.

The Old One folded his wrinkled hands in his lap and asked, "But, surely, not again? Are your ears not tired of listening? Has not this old voice told you these stories more times than there are stars in the heavens?"

Wong Ting's eyes shone with anticipation. "Just once more," he coaxed gently, knowing the Old One wanted to be urged.

Grandfather looked down at Wong Ting a long moment, as if trying to remember how the story started. Impatiently Wong Ting hoped he would hurry, but did not say anything. As he waited, he wished Tsu Li were also here to listen to the tale. He knew Tsu Li would like it.

"In the very beginning," the Old One finally said, smiling his toothless smile, "there were many too poor to buy the land. They did not even have enough coppers to rent a bit of earth to till. It was then they decided to build boat homes. After these were ready, they lived on boats forever after, never again wanting to walk on the land. Content to be river people. Just like we are content to live, and to die, on a sampan."

Yes, thought Wong Ting, Grandfather was right. They were content to be river people. They were all content never to feel the earth beneath their feet, that is, all except himself. But he wisely kept his secret wish locked safely away in his heart.

At this point in the story Grandfather stopped. His faded gray eyes were looking far across the river Wu, as if he could not remember what came next.

"But you forgot the pirates, Grandfather. Tell me about the river pirates," Wong Ting reminded him eagerly.

The Old One pushed his skull cap toward the back of his head and fingered a button on his robe. "It happened when I was exactly your age, eleven Lotus Moons old," he went on. "I was a little taller than my father's shoulder, just as you are. I was helping my father pole our boat toward the City of Min. We had had no warning at all that there were pirates about on the river that day."

When he paused for a breath, Wong Ting quickly prompted, "Yes? Yes?"

The Old One smiled fondly at Wong Ting. Then he continued, "My father had stopped at the docks to pick up two men who wanted to be ferried to a river barge. They were quiet enough during the short trip, but when they were about to step onto the barge, they waved long, curved knives at my father and demanded his money belt. When he did not hurry, they grabbed me by the throat. I can still remember how cold the blade of that knife felt against my skin. I can still remember how I shook with fright."

"Oh, I would have been frightened, too," Wong Ting assured him. "But I have never seen even one river pirate."

"Be glad of that. Heaven smiles on us all. It is not like the days of long ago when I was eleven. Then there was a boat full of robbers for every boat full of good river people."

Their arrival at the market jetty interrupted the Old One's story.

After their sampan was tied to a stout support post, Wong Ting looked toward the land. He sniffed noisily. Besides the smell of fish and freshly cut meat coming from a fishmonger's and a butcher's shop close by, there was a soft perfume in the air. Again he sniffed, liking the delicate odor. Chrysanthemums! These beautiful flowers always blossomed during the Bitter Moon.

Wong Ting smiled to see a fat little man coming away from a bird stall. He was carrying a carved ivory cage almost as big around as himself. In the cage was a brightly plumed singing bird, its long tail feathers a rich blue with splashes of bright gold. Perhaps the bird would sing. Wong Ting waited hopefully, listening for the song. But there was none.

Around the corner a sudden spot of color caught Wong Ting's eyes. As he watched, a sedan chair came into view. A green sedan chair. Why, it could be his Kind Lady. Oh, he hoped so! Then he could thank her for paying the puppeteer.

Ever since that exciting afternoon a few moons ago, Wong Ting had hoped to see her again. Maybe now, in a moment or two, she might come near enough for him to call out his thanks.

As Wong Ting watched, the sedan chair stopped halfway up the market street in front of a trinket shop. A clerk bustled out of the door, bowing low several times. He stood near the small window as if listening to the person hidden behind the green curtain. Scurrying back into his store, he returned almost immediately, holding up a pretty piece of jewelry. The slender hand reached through the small window for the sparkling object, the wide silver bracelet on the arm catching the rays of the sun.

It was his Kind Lady. Wong Ting leaned against the gunwale, breathless with excitement. He was too far away to see the tiny jade dragons, but he knew they were there. If only the four bearers would carry his Kind Lady closer! But they did not. Instead, they picked up the sedan chair, turned around slowly, and moved off down the crowded, winding street. They were soon out of sight.

Although he was disappointed, Wong Ting told himself that he might see her again. Soon perhaps. Then he could tell her how very much he had enjoyed the puppet show.

The bargaining over the day's catch did not take long. Father called out, "Guide us to the Water Gate, my son."

Wong Ting slid onto the steering bench while Lim Sang

untied the ropes that held the boat home against the market jetty. Angling the oar, Wong Ting swung the bow away from the wooden platform. Their sampan turned smoothly in a half circle, finally pointing northward.

As he guided them between the many rafts and junks, Wong Ting wondered why they were headed for the canal above the City of Min. However, he did not have to wait long to find out the reason.

After they entered the narrow waterway that led to the Water Gate, Wong Ting steered between the many boats in the north canal. Because of the strength and quickness of Father's and Lim Sang's poles, their sampan shot ahead on the quiet water.

Before long Wong Ting could see the high arched bridge with its sliding gate, the gate which was always closed at full darkness. These water barriers protected the people in the city from river pirates. No one could enter or leave until daylight returned. Both canals had such a gate.

Wong Ting always enjoyed coming here. He looked forward to seeing this Water Gate. When the sun shone, the high stone arch of the bridge reflected in the still water, forming a complete circle. It made a beautiful picture, as if an artist had brushed each line into place.

As they skimmed under the high arch, Wong Ting was very excited. He now understood why they had come. This was going to be one of those rare happenings—a visit with friends. Just ahead, the orange-colored sampan lay tied to the trunk of an overhanging tree which grew at the edge of the canal.

Excited and happy because he would soon be playing with Tsu Li, Wong Ting watched his brother smiling shyly across the water at the dark-eyed girl in the other boat.

In a short time, they also were tied to the same tree. Father immediately climbed over into the other sampan. Lim Sang followed, climbing swiftly behind him.

Tsu Li, a boy about Wong Ting's size, stepped out of the sleeping cabin surrounded by his small sisters, the giggling three, their pigtails bobbing merrily.

"Hurry, Wong Ting," Tsu Li called out impatiently, "I've something to show you." He stood there near the gunwale, holding a small woven basket in his hands. "A surprise," he went on, his black eyes bright with a teasing look.

"A surprise?" Wong Ting stepped over into the orange-colored sampan. The boys elbowed the giggling sisters out of their way. The girls did not seem to mind this rudeness but stayed close by.

Seeing them right behind him, Tsu Li snapped, "Go 'way. Play Hide-and-Seek or Blind Man or something."

They did not answer him but edged back a few steps, watching the boys and waiting to see what Tsu Li was going to show Wong Ting.

Paying no more attention to them, the boys sat on the mat-covered deck. Tsu Li still held down the lid of the small straw basket. "Guess what I have," he said.

"Marbles," Wong Ting answered quickly, knowing full well if Tsu Li had marbles in the basket, he would not need to hold down the lid. But Wong Ting knew his friend wanted to make a game of guessing.

Tsu Li smiled. "Now, where would a river boy get real marbles?" he demanded. "Only the sons of rich men can find coppers enough to buy marbles. We must content ourselves with stones when we play marbles."

Wong Ting nodded his head, agreeing with his friend. "I'm not much good at guessing," Wong Ting went on, "but could you, do you have—crickets?"

Tsu Li grinned. "My friend, who is like a brother to me, is very good at guessing. That's just what I do have. One cricket for me and one for you. We're going to race them."

Wong Ting was excited. "That will be fun," he said, "but where did you ever get them? Surely they did not jump into your boat?"

Laughing good naturedly, Tsu Li explained, "Of course not. The market man at our jetty gave them to me. I told him once that I'd like to race crickets with my friend, Wong Ting, but river boys had no way of finding them since these insects live on the land."

"That is true," Wong Ting agreed.

"So, yesterday," Tsu Li continued, "he had these for me in this basket." He turned to glower at his sisters. "One of them broke the catch on this basket sometime this morning while I was busy poling. I wish I knew which one did it. I would—" His serious black eyes stared at the little girls a moment. Seeing his anger, they no longer smiled, but they stood their ground, not budging an inch.

Shrugging, Tsu Li turned to look at Wong Ting. "The market man," Tsu Li went on, "also gave me some light string to tie them up. I could hardly wait until I saw you."

For a moment, a sudden boldness overtook Wong Ting, seeing the closeness of the land. Without thinking, he blurted out, "Maybe we could find more crickets ourselves. Over there, on the land."

A look of disbelief crossed Tsu Li's face. "My ears play tricks on me," he said slowly. "What madness is this? You cannot mean you want to walk on the land?"

Wong Ting sighed. It was no use. Not even his best friend could understand this desire of his to feel the earth beneath his padded shoes.

"Your ears do not know teasing when they hear it," Wong Ting hastened to say. "Come, let us race our crickets."

It did not take the boys long to knot an end of string around the body of each of the small black crickets.

"Now they cannot hop out of the boat," Tsu Li said.

Being the visitor, Wong Ting was given his choice of the insects. He looked down at them. They were so much alike that he had a hard time trying to decide which one he wanted. Picking up the cricket closest to him, he said, "This is the one I will race," and tied two knots in the end of the string so he would be able to recognize which cricket belonged to him.

A few rules were agreed upon, and the fun began. So intent upon their game were Tsu Li and Wong Ting that they did not notice the giggling sisters had come closer. They were breathing down the necks of the boys, so anxious were they to see the racing.

Looking up, Tsu Li said crossly, "Did I not tell you to go away?"

His mother stood in the cabin doorway. She must have heard his words, for she chided him softly. "Do not be selfish, my son. The girls do no harm. No one on this boat has ever seen crickets race. Let them stay."

Tsu Li shook his head resignedly. The giggling three became bolder and stepped closer.

"You should be glad there are no sisters on your sampan," Tsu Li said.

Wong Ting was so interested in the races, he had not been listening to the talk of the men. They sat on benches at the stern.

However, Wong Ting stopped the game long enough to listen to Tsu Li's father. "It is true, Father of Sons," he said, speaking directly to Wong Ting's father. "I tell you, river people are being robbed ..."

Wong Ting looked anxiously at the group. The Old One had cupped a hand behind his ear. He asked, "Eh? You say river pirates?"

Tsu Li's father spoke even louder to make himself heard by

the old man. "Yes, river pirates. For the past two moons there have been robbers on the Wu. It is said, by those who know, that these brigands have a six-oared boat. They are swift—too swift for us with our sails and poles. My friend would have been caught by them this very morning had not the fog closed in, hiding his sampan from their greedy eyes."

Wong Ting felt the hopelessness in Father's answer. "River pirates, again? That is all this family needs."

Tsu Li's father went on. "Do not despair, Father of Sons. It is easy to recognize their boat. There is an ugly red devil fish carved on the high prow. By that you will know them."

"Eh? A red devil fish you say?" Father sounded eager. "Listen to that, my second son. Your eyes are as sharp as an eagle's. Did you not find us an anchor stone? I hope your eyes will warn us in time if pirates row upon our river."

Wong Ting smiled. "I will see the devil boat long before it sees us," he boasted.

Tsu Li said impatiently, "Is it pirates we are interested in, or cricket racing? The red devil fish won't come now."

Before Wong Ting could answer, both mothers appeared in the doorway to the cabin. The food was ready. Eagerly the men stood up and went inside the small, roofed room. Wong Ting wished they would hurry. His stomach was growling for rice.

While they waited, the boys continued to race their crickets. So far Tsu Li's had won five races, while Wong Ting's had beaten only three times.

Before long the women and children were seated around the large bowl of steaming food. Wong Ting held his chopsticks in his right hand. In his left he had a small china dish. He held this close to his chin to keep the hot juices from dripping on the matting or on his padded trousers.

As he ate, Wong Ting grunted aloud at the deliciousness of the food. Pink shrimp could be seen hiding here and there among the softened grains of brown rice. He ran his tongue around the edges of his mouth in between bites, to lose none of the flavor. He smacked his lips again and again to show how much he was enjoying it. They all smacked their lips and grunted aloud at such a feast.

Wong Ting noticed that the shrimp were fast disappearing from the big dish. He would have liked to lift out more for himself, but he must not be impolite. Had not his mother said, "Eat slowly when we are at rice with friends. Do not be the first to pick out what you like the best."

Remembering her words, Wong Ting stopped his chopsticks to look out through the opened door. With quick little glances, he watched the many boats skimming past them on the canal. This helped to slow his eating.

As he looked at the land, so close yet so far away from him, his secret wish came back into his thoughts, filling his heart with a hopeless longing. He asked himself if it was foolishness in him to dream this dream. Was it madness as Tsu Li just said for Wong Ting to want to walk on the land? No! He did not agree with his friend. Wong Ting saw no harm in his secret wish. Some day he knew this dream would come true if he only kept on dreaming it.

After they had eaten all of the rice they could hold, there were little round almond cakes and tiny bowls filled to the brim with hot, fragrant tea. The delicious drink warmed Wong Ting clear down to the tips of his pointed cloth shoes.

After their stomachs were so full they could not swallow another sip of tea, Tsu Li jumped to his feet. "Come along, Wong Ting," he said. "Let's get back to our racing."

But his mother said, "There will be no time for games. We are going to have a treat for our ears."

Tsu Li sat down again, disappointment in his face. The men came back into the cabin to listen to the dark-eyed girl. She stood near the door, waiting for the giggling three to quiet down. Then she sang songs to them in a high, sweet voice.

Wong Ting enjoyed the lively melodies very much. He had heard them before. River people knew them well.

While she sang, the dark-eyed girl kept looking out from under her long lashes at Lim Sang, who smiled back at her.

The stars crept into the darkened sky, and the Bitter Moon was shining brightly before the singing had ended. Sleepily Wong Ting heard the polite words spoken in thanks and the good wishes said as his family climbed back into their own sampan.

Wong Ting lay awake for a while, thinking about this visit with Tsu Li. In the morning after the Water Gate opened, both families would pole out of the canal to the fishing grounds, but there would still be the pleasant memory of this evening to keep with them always.

Yawning sleepily, Wong Ting turned over and pillowed his head on his arms. Soon he was dreaming about ugly river pirates riding big, jade dragons.

Chapter 5:
The Fire

All through the Budding Moon the fishing continued to be good. Here and there on the river Wu, small, white-edged waves formed and broke against the boats, whipped into action by the first gusts of a coming storm.

One morning Father looked at the low hanging clouds. "Tonight," he predicted, "the Winds of Heaven will blow hard. We will anchor in the harbor, tying ourselves to the sampans on either side of us to keep from overturning."

That evening after third rice, they dropped their anchor stone close to the City of Min. The wind had quieted somewhat. Wong Ting hoped it had blown itself out over the South China Sea where it would do little damage.

Later, he lay on his sleeping mat, dreaming about a big devil fish riding in a bright red sedan chair. Upon its flat head sat a narrow bamboo crown. Dancing along the edge were ten dragons, exactly like the jade dragons in his Kind Lady's bracelet, only these were not green in color, but red.

Suddenly something awakened Wong Ting. Had the dawn come already? Had he slept the darkness away? He looked up sleepily at the curved roof, blinking hard, trying to drive away that silly dream. As he watched, the ceiling of the small cabin turned a bright red. He heard the roar of flames close by and felt the stifling heat of fire.

Wong Ting rolled off his sleeping mat. He hurried across the small room to waken his family. He shook Father by the shoulder, calling out in a loud voice, "Get up, everyone. Fire! Fire!"

Father was awake in an instant. A moment later, the others struggled sleepily to their feet. Soon they all stood on the deck, looking across the harbor toward the City of Min. Many buildings were already in flames.

Father said, "We need all hands at the poles. There are some who may need our help."

Almost at once their boat was free of its ropes. Wong Ting steered while the men pushed with their poles.

The wind suddenly blew harder. Wong Ting saw a junk close to the wharf turn red as hot sparks dropped on its dry, wooden decks. Soon smoke hid it from sight.

By now the air was so full of ashes Wong Ting could hardly breathe, and his eyes stung, causing them to water. He rubbed the sleeve of his padded coat across them in order to see.

This night would never be forgotten by Wong Ting. As he steered closer to those who might need their help, he knew that many would die, for few boatmen could swim.

As he looked ahead, the walls of the tallow factory crumbled, sending up sparks and ashes. River people, screaming with fear, leaped from their flaming boats. Other families began dragging the unfortunates from the river.

Wong Ting kept hoping that they would be able to rescue someone. But he could not steer any closer to the shore. There were too many boats in front of theirs.

Loud cries filled the air, and out in the darkness behind them, a dog barked. He sounded unhappy and afraid. Wong Ting hoped the animal was not lost from his river family.

The wind changed direction again. Hot ashes now fell all around their boat home. One large flake touched Wong Ting's cheek. He could feel the skin burn where it had fallen. The warmth of the blazing fire was almost too hot to bear. Beads of perspiration formed on his brow and rolled down his face. His throat felt dry and ached from the stifling air.

Father kept brushing ashes off his shoulders. "It is better that we steer out of this," he said. "If there are any who need our help, we will be close enough to pick them up."

Wong Ting was bitterly disappointed, but he knew that these words held wisdom. Their own sampan might catch on fire if they stayed so near to the leaping flames. Father was sensible enough not to let that happen to them.

Again Wong Ting swerved toward the middle of the Wu, gripping the steering oar in his tired fingers. He kept looking across the dark water for the white splashes that would show a man, woman, or a child floundering in the river. But, no matter how carefully he watched, he saw no one.

Oh, how he hoped that those in the orange-colored sampan had not chosen to anchor in the harbor this night! How he hoped Tsu Li and all of the others were far away from the fury of this fire.

The Winds of Heaven were now blowing harder. Just when Wong Ting thought the flames had gone out, they burst into new tongues of yellow and red. Each new spurt of wind helped to keep the fire alive.

Not far away Wong Ting could see an old man being pulled into a boat. His padded coat and trousers were so heavy with water that the men had a hard time getting him over the gunwale. Not until the two women on that boat home added their strength to that of the men was the unfortunate one rescued from the cold, dark river.

Next, a half-grown child was being helped into another sampan. Wong Ting wished that they, too, could aid someone. But, before these homeless ones reached the far edge of the mass of boats, where they were, some other river family had pulled them to safety.

Father waited until the last glow from the fire had died out. The night was more than half over when he told Wong Ting to steer back to the other side of the harbor where they had been anchored before. Soon they were safely tied to the boats on either side of them.

Again the family went back to their sleeping mats. Then it became quiet. Wong Ting had a hard time getting back to his dreams, for his eyes and throat still felt dry and scratchy from the smoky air. But he turned over and pillowed his head on his arms. Resolutely, he tried to forget this night's sad happening, but he could not. The horror of the scenes he had just witnessed kept him wide awake.

After a while Wong Ting heard a faint noise. As he lay still, listening, he heard it a second time. Then again and again. It sounded like the whimpering of a baby.

Wong Ting tiptoed across the cabin to the corner where the Last Born slept. Leaning down, Wong Ting put an ear close to the baby's face. It had not been his little brother, for he was fast asleep.

The sound must have come from the river. Squeezing past the bamboo curtain across the doorway, Wong Ting walked along the deck and leaned far out over the gunwale near the bow. It was then that he heard a small splashing sound. Then someone whimpered. A baby must be in the river. But that was not possible. All of the people had been picked up long ago. Had they not waited until the fire was out before returning to their sleeping mats?

Yet in front of Wong Ting there was a sound of splashing. By now his eyes were used to the darkness. He saw something floating in the river. A child. It was a child no bigger than the Last Born. The baby was crying quietly, as if he had been crying quite some time and could not cry hard any longer.

As the baby bobbed about in the river, Wong Ting could see

four or five big gourds tied about the small waist. These kept the baby up high in the water.

The splashing sound that Wong Ting had heard had been made by a little black dog. He was swimming around and around the baby as if to protect him from danger.

Wong Ting wondered why the child had not been seen by someone long before this. But he was glad it had happened just this way. Now he could rescue him.

Leaning far out, holding on with one hand, Wong Ting coaxed, "Take my hand. Soon you'll be dry and warm."

The child stared, his upper lip trembling as if he would begin crying again.

Wong Ting watched the direction of the current. It would bring him the baby in a few minutes. Soon Wong Ting's fingers touched the small arm. Then his hands grabbed hold of the soggy clothing. He lifted with all of his strength. The dripping baby was soon standing on the deck, crying softly.

Wong Ting leaned out over the gunwale once more for the little dog who was soon jumping up on the child, barking joyfully. The noise awakened the family.

"What is this?" Father asked, stumbling sleepily through the door.

Mother asked no questions. She lifted the baby in her arms and carried him into the warmth of the sleeping room.

"Drop the curtains, Wong Ting," she said when they were all inside the sleeping room.

Wong Ting unrolled the bamboo matting, tying it snugly at the bottom to keep the cold air out.

Mother was holding the small hands of the rescued child in her larger ones. "He's so cold, so cold," she said. "He must have been in the Wu a long, long time."

They sat around, watching her as she stripped off the wet clothes and dried the child on some clean rags. Then she

wrapped him in a warm cover she took from her own mat.
From a bowl she fed him cold food left over from third rice.
Even the little dog ate greedily, as if it had been a long time
since someone had offered him something to eat.

Father leaned down to look into the baby's face. "What's your
name?" Father asked.

There was no answer. The child stared at Father with large,
solemn eyes.

"Enough of questions," Mother said, lifting the little boy and
putting him down on the edge of Wong Ting's sleeping mat.
"He needs rest. To bed, all of you. Tomorrow is time enough for
questions."

Father grumbled, then spoke of his plans. "We will ask the
river people who this child is. We will then return him to
his parents."

"Wong Ting," Mother said, "hold the baby close to your
warmth. Try to get him to sleep. He will soon forget the fire and
the hours he spent in the river. Babies have short memories."

Wong Ting snuggled under his coverings, pulling the boy
against him. The dog lay down beside the baby.

For a while Wong Ting could feel the shivers going through
the body of the child, but in a short time, even before Wong
Ting fell asleep, the baby quieted.

This time Wong Ting was too tired to dream, and the light of
dawn came too soon. When he awakened, he tucked the covers
around the little boy who still slept soundly.

As he poled, Wong Ting began to think about the child he
had rescued. Who could he be? By now his family must be truly
worried about him.

Later in the morning, as they passed each boat, Father
cried out, "He la, ho la! Good day and good fishing! Do you
know this boy?" And he held up the child so that he could be
plainly seen.

Each time there came the same answer. "We have never before looked upon that boy."

They delayed their fishing long enough to stay close to the harbor at the City of Min where the child had been rescued, hoping to find his parents.

Again and again Father called out, "Good day and good fishing. Do you know this boy?"

After first rice was over, an old woman in a large sampan nodded her head at the question. "I know him," she admitted, "but my tongue is slow to speak what I know."

"Out with it, Woman," Father said, his voice full of impatience. "I wish to return him to his parents. Where are they?"

All hope of giving him back to his family was gone as she answered, "His father and mother can no longer grieve for him."

"Were they lost?" Father asked.

"Yes." The old woman shook her head sadly. "Theirs was one of the last sampans to catch on fire."

In the dreadful silence that followed, everyone stood looking down at the small boy. He was busy patting his little dog, jabbering happily, too young to understand the tragic words just spoken.

Wong Ting stooped down to throw an arm about him. "Isn't it sad," Wong Ting said shyly. "He has no father or mother. No brother or sisters. He is all alone except for his dog."

"Was the whole family lost?" Father insisted, wanting to be sure.

"All! All except for him. But how is he saved?"

"A belt of gourds held him up high in the river," Father explained. Sighing deeply, as if realizing what this meant to them all, he went on, "I am not sure whether or not Heaven smiles or frowns on us this day, but one thing is certain—this family now has a new Little Brother."

A new Little Brother. A Little Brother from the river!

As Wong Ting repeated these words to himself, his heart filled with gladness. Already he loved this little boy. Out of this sad happening would come happiness, Wong Ting felt sure. Had not Mother said babies have short memories? Perhaps Little Brother would remember nothing except his life with them on this sampan.

The child smiled suddenly. Reaching up, he put his hand into Wong Ting's larger one, as if he understood he now belonged to them.

Chapter 6:
The Winds of Heaven

The next night, after third rice, Mother made a bed for the new brother next to the Last Born. Little Brother lay very still where she placed him, as if content.

She stood above the little boys and smiled sweetly. "He's such a good baby," she said. "No trouble at all."

Father groaned wearily as he threw the cover over himself. He sounded cross when he grumbled, "Humph! Another mouth to feed. Don't forget that."

Wong Ting looked anxiously from Father to Mother and back again, studying their solemn faces. Would Father give the boy away because there might not be enough rice?

Mother's reply made Wong Ting's worries disappear. She offered in her quiet, gentle way, "Yes, my husband, what you say is true. It is another mouth to fill. But soon there will be another pair of hands to help with the fishing and a strong young back to help with the poling when yours is weak with age."

After their sampan had quieted, Wong Ting felt a warm ball of softness crawling under his covers. Before he could wake up fully, Little Brother had rolled against him, sighed deeply, and closed his eyes in sleep. The dog, too, was soon breathing deeply, rolled into a ball next to the child.

Wong Ting wondered if he should put the baby back on his own mat next to the Last Born. What would Mother say in the morning when she found Little Brother beside him? Wong Ting yawned sleepily. The child probably missed his family.

Several times during the next few days the Winds of Heaven blew hard, with strange periods of quiet in between.

This morning Father stopped his poling to look up thoughtfully at the heavy clouds. He seemed worried.

When Lim Sang asked him about the coming storm, Father answered, "It feels like monsoon weather. The air is getting heavy with moisture."

The next day Wong Ting awakened to the heavy slap of waves against the wooden sides of the sampan. The wind was whipping the river into angry swirls. He was glad that they were tied snugly to the boats on each side of them.

By the time the first rice was over, however, the wind had blown itself out; at least, that is what Father said, and added, "We go to the fishing grounds." They untied the ropes and were on their way.

But Father was mistaken. The quiet period did not last long. Scarcely had they dropped their fishing net when the Winds of Heaven started in again. Wong Ting wished they were still safely in the harbor, but they were far upstream.

Even before their soggy net could be pulled out of the Wu the rain began, slowly at first, then faster and faster. In a short time, Wong Ting could not see the land; the grey wall of water shut them in. Only their sampan and a bit of angry river could be seen.

Father called out to Mother, who stood in the doorway holding the little boys by the hand. "Keep the children inside. Fasten the curtain. Hurry!" Then he said, "Up with the net."

All hands pulled hard on the water-soaked netting. Inch by inch, as they pulled and pulled, the heavy webbing piled up on the deck.

As Lim Sang began to heave the net up onto the cabin roof, Father shouted, "Leave it. There is more important work for our strength. Dig in with your poles."

The tug of the tide surprised and worried Wong Ting. He had never felt it this strong before. It was as if they did not use their poles at all. In spite of the forceful way they dug in, the Winds of Heaven kept pushing them faster and faster downstream. If this continued, they might be dashed into the bay of Wang— perhaps even into the South China Sea.

It proved to be a real struggle with only three stout poles against the fury of the storm. The City of Min slid by so fast they could not turn into the harbor where they would have found safety. But they were swept by too rapidly. Although the Old One angled the steering oar in plenty of time, the swirling current held them out in the middle of the raging Wu.

A little later, Father cupped his hands about his mouth to shout toward the stern. "We will try for the south canal."

From his place at the bow, Wong Ting could see better than the others. Besides, were not his eyes as sharp as an eagle's? Several times it was on the tip of his tongue to tell Father that they had drifted far below the south canal. But if Wong Ting should tell what he knew, there would be no hope left. Unless the Fortune of Heaven helped them, they would soon be swept down into the ocean.

They all tired quickly from the great effort of trying to stop the swift tide from pulling them along so rapidly. The strength of three was not enough. Even if they had ten more men to help them, or twenty or forty, they would be no match for the force of the wind and the tug of the tide.

A boat as small as theirs could not hope to ride safely upon the high waves of the South China Sea. Indeed, they might capsize long before they reach the ocean. By now the Winds of Heaven had so strengthened the tide that a pole was as a twig in a man's hand.

Wong Ting could not say to Father or Lim Sang, "There is no hope for us. We have drifted beyond our last chance of being saved."

Although these dark thoughts filled Wong Ting's heart with despair, he kept right on holding firm, gripping the pole with all his strength. Grimly he set his lips tightly together to prevent them from speaking out what he knew.

As Wong Ting dug in his pole, he squinted, trying to see through the heavy downpour, but it completely shut out the high banks along the edges of the Wu.

Something began to stir in Wong Ting's memory. It stayed far back in his mind, a vague shadow of a thought. He tried to grasp what it was, puckering his brow. After a while he remembered. Unless his memory played a trick on him, it had happened on the same day Wong Ting had found the new anchor stone—only earlier. There had been an irrigation ditch in the middle of a field of young cabbage plants. Had not Father said it was about as wide as the north canal? With the skillful steering of the Old One, their sampan might be able to get into that ditch out of the storm's path.

Wong Ting decided not to speak about this until they neared the place. Occasionally there was a brief clearing between the gusts of rain, during which he caught a glimpse of the land. He kept watching for the irrigation ditch, digging in with his pole and holding as firmly as he could.

They were all soaking wet and shivering with the cold, but Wong Ting felt sorrier for the Old One who steered. The icy wind must be chilling him clear to his bones.

At last when Wong Ting saw what he hoped to see, his teeth chattered with the cold, making words hard to speak.

"F-f-fa-ther," he yelled above the din of the storm. "S-s-s-ee? T-the d-ditch."

Father must have understood what Wong Ting was trying to tell him. He and Lim Sang dug in firmly, swinging the bow landward. Even the Old One must have grasped what was meant. He began to scull frantically until Wong Ting felt the boat twisting directly under his feet. It leaped ahead toward the mouth of the irrigation ditch.

When their bow crashed up against the thick wooden gate, Wong Ting was thrown against the gunwale. He almost fell into the water, but saved himself by grabbing hold of the bow.

Father roared, "Quick, Lim Sang. The wheel! Turn it!"

Lim Sang leaped into the air, grabbing hold of the top of the big wheel. The weight of his long, man-length body pulled it downward.

Wong Ting heard the sharp, creaking sound it made as the gate began to open. He was so excited that he nearly forgot to pull hard on his pole to keep them from being sucked back into the black, swirling river.

As Wong Ting watched, Lim Sang leaped again and again, each time riding the big wheel down until his feet touched the deck once more.

The opening was growing larger and larger. Now it was large enough for them to slide under. Wong Ting felt the raging river lifting the stern. It picked up the sampan as if it were a leaf and tossed it into the ditch. They floated a short distance on the shallow water.

Wong Ting was surprised to hear Father say, "Be quick, Lim Sang. Drop the gate."

They were quite safe. Why did Father want the opening closed?

Again and again his big brother jumped high into the air. The wheel turned backwards slowly. Soon the wooden gate was in place, shutting off the river that had been rushing into the ditch.

They all rested where they were, as if not believing they had been saved from the fury of the storm.

Father's next words explained his reason for closing the ditch. "It would be dishonorable to allow the land to be flooded," he said. "The crops would be ruined. Many hungry mouths would go unfilled."

As he listened to these wise words, Wong Ting wished with all of his heart that every other river family would find a place of safety to hide from the monsoon.

Lim Sang was standing close to the bow, staring glumly at the land. His voice shook when he asked, "Do you suppose, Father, they are...all right?"

Father shrugged wearily. "If the Fortune of Heaven smiles on them this day..." He did not finish the sentence, but they all knew what he meant.

Wong Ting hoped that the orange-colored sampan rode at anchor along the quiet waters of the north canal. He hoped Tsu Li, his parents, and sisters had found a place of safety during the storm.

Too tired to eat, Wong Ting crawled under his covers. As soon as his head touched his sleeping mat, he slept.

Chapter 7:
Wong Ting, Ferryman

In the dim grayness of dawn, the morning after they had
found safety from the monsoon, Wong Ting stood silently in
the bow of the sampan. He stared thoughtfully at the straight
furrows cut into the dark, rich earth on both sides of the
irrigation ditch.

Wong Ting kept toying with an idea. The land was so close
that he knew he could jump from the deck onto it in one quick
leap. Yet he hesitated, knowing full well the dismay this would
cause his family. The Winds of Heaven had already filled their
hearts with unhappiness and worry over the damage this storm
had left behind.

No! Wong Ting decided he would not walk on the land.
Not now! Later on, perhaps, but not today. This was certainly
no time to add to Father's burdens by doing what river people
scorned to do. Wong Ting would wait, and some day, he hoped,
there would be a right moment to make his wish come true. In
the meantime, he'd be patient, and he would keep on dreaming
his dream.

After first rice Lim Sang again opened and closed the thick,
wooden gate at the mouth of the waterway. The rain had
stopped during the night, and the Winds of Heaven had blown
themselves out. The river Wu was quiet at last.

As they poled upstream, Wong Ting saw many smashed
sampans drifting upside down on top of the water. These pieces

of wreckage meant that many river people had lost their lives during the monsoon. Wong Ting held the constant hope in his heart that the orange-colored sampan had found a place of safety away from the churning waves and the icy winds. He yearned for a glimpse of Tsu Li's smiling face and to feel again the friendly clasp of his hand.

Lim Sang bent to his poling, but his mouth was set in a grim, tight line. Wong Ting saw the sadness in his brother's eyes because of the worries over the dark-eyed girl and her family. Though Lim Sang did not speak about them, Wong Ting knew that there would be no smile on his brother's lips until the orange-colored sampan came into view.

Before dawn the next day, while the sun still slept, Mother shook Wong Ting gently by the shoulder to awaken him from his dreams.

"Come," she urged, "the fever burns within your father's body. Lim Sang moans with his pain, and the skin of the Old One is also hot to the touch. Yesterday's long hard poling against the current and the storm's icy dampness proved too much for them. You must be the man of this family until the sick become well."

A frightening thought filled Wong Ting's heart. He asked anxiously, "What about the Last Born and Little Brother?"

"They still sleep. I felt no fever in them, not once during the whole of the night."

Stepping out onto the deck, Wong Ting began to think about what he should do. If he was going to be the man of this family until the sick became well, he would have to earn some coins. Hungry mouths could not go unfilled, especially the mouths of those who were weak with fever.

Wong Ting could not catch fish by himself. Two pairs of hands could not pole upstream against the current. It took more than two pairs of hands to raise and lower the heavy net. Besides, he could not count on his mother's help. She was needed in the sleeping cabin. Hot faces had to be sponged with cool river water. Food had to be prepared. Yes, there were many tasks awaiting her.

Wong Ting sat down on the bench near the door of the sleeping cabin. Surely there must be a way he could earn the needed coppers. As he leaned back against the stout bamboo mast, he was busy with his thoughts. At the back of his mind, the words of the Old One came back to him. In those stories about the river people, Grandfather had said again and again, "I was helping my father pole our boat toward the City of Min. My father had stopped at the docks to pick up two men who wanted to be ferried to the river barge."

Wong Ting smiled at this memory. Why couldn't he be a ferryman? His great-grandfather had been a ferryman. Many families who owned large sampans earned their rice by taking passengers to the river steamers. Why not he? Even if their boat was small, Wong Ting could manage one or two customers each trip. The money belt would probably not sag with heaviness should he turn ferryman. However, he should be able to earn enough coins for the food that was needed.

Mother caught him pulling up the anchor stone. "What is this son doing?" she asked gently.

"Has not the Old One told me about his father being a ferryman? I will try to find some who wish to be taken to the steamer. Perhaps I can earn enough coins for the things that will be needed."

She smiled at him and patted his shoulder. "Since you are to be the man of this family until the sick become well," she said gently, "it is for you to decide what is to be done."

At her words a proud, happy feeling came over Wong Ting. He felt grown-up enough to do the work of a man.

"Keep the babies inside the cabin," Wong Ting said. "I

will need the space on the deck for my passengers and
their luggage."

Mother looked closely at him, then nodded her head. "It
will be done," she answered with quiet dignity, as if she were
answering an order given by her husband.

This quick agreement to his wishes made Wong Ting feel
much older than his eleven years. He felt confident that he
could be the man of the family for as long as necessary.

Poling straight toward the wharf at the harbor of the City
of Min, Wong Ting noticed the blackened ruins of the tallow
factory and the other buildings burned in the fire. The sight of
these broken walls reminded him again of that dreadful night
during the Bitter Moon. But something wonderful had happened
on the night of the fire. Wong Ting had found Little Brother.

When the bow of their sampan scraped against a stout
support beam near a long flight of wooden steps, Wong Ting
reached out to take hold of the post. Above him on the high
dock stood many people. Several carried big boxes. Others bird
cages. Maybe one of these travelers would give him a chance to
ferry him across the river Wu.

"He la, ho la," Wong Ting called out. "This sampan will take
you to the river steamer. And quickly, too. Is there one who
needs a ferry?"

Several men looked down at the small boat, nudging each
other and laughing. A tall traveler said scornfully, "See the small
man-child who wants to be a ferryman."

Another shouted, "Such skinny arms. They are no match for
the long pole."

Wong Ting felt anger rise within him. But he must not show
his feelings. This was no way to coax passengers.

Paying no attention to these impolite words, Wong Ting tried
once more, calling out as cheerfully as he could manage, "Is
there one who wants a ferry?"

A thin man with a long white beard pushed his way to the front of the crowd. He looked at least as old as Wong Ting's grandfather.

"Eh?" he said, in a voice shaky with age. "Did I hear an offer of a ferryman?"

Wong Ting clung to the edge of the wharf, smiling up at the Ancient One above him on the high dock. "Oh yes, Honored Sir," Wong Ting replied politely, hopefully. "I will take you to the steamer, and quickly, too."

The old man seemed to be thinking over Wong Ting's words. Then he asked, "The price, Young Ferryman? What will you charge for your services?"

"What it is worth to you, Honored Sir," Wong Ting answered, not quite knowing how much to charge for the trip.

Satisfied, the Ancient One began to clump down the stairs, bumping a large box at every step. Wong Ting steadied the sampan as his first customer, dragging his box, climbed in slowly.

Then a second man, fully as old, came down the stairway. "I will pay what it is worth," he promised.

When they were both safely seated on the bench in front of the cabin door, Wong Ting shoved off, glad that Mother was keeping the children inside and out of the way.

The lifting and pushing began and continued steadily. Wong Ting felt thankful that yesterday's storm had not left high waves or a strong tide.

The hard, steady poling went on and on until the dark shadow across the water ahead of him showed Wong Ting that the river steamer was close by. He turned the sampan so that it would glide along the far side where rope ladders hung over the gunwale. This was a strange way for travelers to get up to the deck of the big ship so high above them.

Wong Ting's passengers acted as if they were used to such climbing ropes. They did not hesitate.

As the first customer stood up, he asked, "The price? What is the price, Young Ferryman?"

Wong Ting gave the same answer as before, "What it is worth to you, Honored Sir."

The two old men put their heads together to whisper a moment, then each one handed Wong Ting two shiny coppers. This was much more than he had expected them to pay.

Gratefully, he said, "I was pleased to serve you."

He clung to the rope ladder as his passengers began the ascent. Two husky sailors reached over for their boxes. Others grabbed hold of their arms, helping them more quickly to the deck of the steamer.

When they were safely on board, they both leaned over the railing to wave at Wong Ting. He waved back and called up another thank you.

Through the long hours of daylight, Wong Ting made his way between the harbor and the middle of the river. As he poled, he daydreamed about his secret wish and felt envious of his customers because they could walk on the land.

As the sampan skimmed over the water, Wong Ting kept a sharp lookout upstream and downstream for a glimpse of the orange-colored sampan. For Tsu Li and the giggling three. For all of them. They were almost as dear to Wong Ting as his own family. If only the Fortune of Heaven smiled on them, too!

When the sun finally hid itself behind the rooftops of the City of Min, Wong Ting smelled the good odor of food cooking in the cabin. He grinned happily. He was tired, of course, and his arms ached clear to his shoulders. But in the money belt there were enough coins to barter for the family's needs.

On the third day of ferrying passengers, Wong Ting rested a moment on his pole to ease his breathing. A brightness far upriver caught his attention. Could it be …? Yes, it was! There was no mistaking the orange-colored sampan. At each stroke of the poles it was moving farther and farther away, headed for the fishing grounds above the north canal.

Wong Ting shouted happily, "Come quickly, my mother."

When she hurried to his side, he pointed up the Wu with an eager finger. "Is that not the dark-eyed girl who waves at us? Tell my sick brother."

Mother smiled her gentle smile. "Your eyes are as sharp as an eagle's," she replied. "It is the orange-colored sampan. I will go to tell your brother. His fever will cool quickly now that they are safe, too."

Wong Ting's heart beat fast with gladness when he saw three little figures in the bow and a taller one close by—Tsu Li and his giggling sisters.

They were safe. Heaven had smiled on them, too. Their boat home had found a place to hide from the fury of the great storm.

Several days later, even before the anchor stone had been pulled from the Wu, Father sat on his bed mat. His face was still white and drawn from the weakness. However, he did look much better. He held his chopsticks above a small eating bowl.

Smiling across the cabin, he asked, "What is this your mother tells me, Wong Ting? About being a ferryman?"

Wong Ting told what he had done while the fever burned within those who were ill.

Father kept interrupting him, wanting to know the details of each day's trips. He asked question after question until at last he seemed satisfied with the answers.

Wong Ting almost burst with pride when Father boomed out for all to hear, "It is a wonderful, grown-up thing this son has done." Patting the money belt about his waist, he added, "And, thanks to Wong Ting, there were coppers enough to feed us all."

These words pleased Wong Ting. He could hardly wait until they poled upriver to the fishing grounds where Tsu Li's family went each day. When Wong Ting was close enough to shout at his friend, he would tell Tsu Li about being the man of the family and how he had earned the food for hungry mouths by being a ferryman.

Chapter 8:
River Pirates

The fragrance of the Peony Moon was at last upon the land. Wong Ting sniffed at the spring air filled with the perfume of blossoming trees. Here and there he saw patches of new, glossy tea leaves shining darkly on the distant hillsides, ready for first picking.

In the fields along both banks of the Wu, rice paddies would soon take the place of the winter wheat that had just been harvested. Wong Ting watched the hard-working farmers bending to the task of setting out the seedlings that had been growing in the nursery beds. He knew that before long the slow-moving buffalo would be pulling plows through the dark earth.

Two months had passed since the fever had gone, yet father often complained at his continuing weakness.

To soothe his crossness, Mother promised, "Soon, my husband, your arms will push on the pole with the same strength as before. Do not be impatient."

Now that Lim Sang and Father handled the work of poling, Wong Ting found himself more and more at the steering oar. Ever since his sickness, the Old One coughed and coughed whenever he sat too long in the damp morning air. After the sun came out, however, he always appeared on deck to help with the fishing, in spite of the urging of the others that he rest inside the warm cabin just a little longer.

Wong Ting often snatched a moment to play with the Last Born and Little Brother and the dog. The babies played happily, chatting words understood by only themselves. Wherever the Last Born crawled, there also came Little Brother, a small, quick shadow behind him. If the Last Born pulled himself up against the gunwale to dabble his hand into the river, there also climbed Little Brother.

Often their ropes tangled about their ankles. When this happened both jabbered excitedly while the dog ran around them in circles. The family laughed merrily, watching the little boys trying to unwind themselves. When the knots tightened, Wong Ting straightened them out, then returned to his work.

This morning, as soon as they began to fish, Wong Ting's thoughts were far away. He was thinking about his Kind Lady and her beautiful silver bracelet. Wong Ting would never forget how the jade dragons danced when her arm moved. Many times he wished that she could have heard his thanks on that afternoon of the puppet show. He wanted her to know how much he had enjoyed seeing it.

As Wong Ting looked toward the shore, he thought about his secret wish. With each passing day, his longing to walk on the land grew stronger and stronger. He would never lose his yearning until he felt the earth beneath his padded shoes. He did not quite know how he was going to manage to do this without making his family think he did not want to be a boatman. But he did! Just like all river people, he loved the Wu, feeling great pity for those who must be forever chained to the land.

Toward the middle of the day, a great commotion began among the river families. Hands were eagerly pulling up nets, even though there were still many fishing hours left. Soon they poled rapidly downstream toward the City of Min.

Could pirates be on the Wu? Had the six-oared boat come to

rob them? Anxiously Wong Ting looked upstream, sighing with relief when he saw no boat with a red devil fish on the prow.

Wong Ting heard Father say, "Pull up our net. We go to see what is happening. Come Wong Ting, pole swiftly."

They poled downstream until they were close to the harbor. When they had to slow down because of the hundreds and hundreds of sampans all around them, Father called out, "He la, ho la," trying to attract someone's attention.

"He la, ho la," he called again and again, but the river people were so busy throwing fish nets into the muddy Wu, they did not trouble to answer his greeting.

Mother was more successful. She listened a while to the chatter of the women on the nearest boat. Then she explained, "It is not fish for which they fish. Toss in our net, my husband. Be quick! The wife of a rich merchant lost her bracelet at moon time last night, right about here. While leaving the steamer, it became loosened from her arm. Three jade dragons dangle from a wide silver bracelet."

"Eh?" Father grunted. "Three dragons, you say? Jade dragons?"

Jade dragons! Three jade dragons! Wong Ting's thoughts flew back to the day of the box theater. To the bright green sedan chair. To his Kind Lady. She had worn such a bracelet. He would never forget it. There had been three dragons on it—jade dragons. Could it be possible that this bracelet which was lost in the river was hers? It must be hers. Wong Ting doubted that there was another such bracelet in all of China—in all of the world.

If only he could find it for her! If that happened, Wong Ting would ask permission to take it to her. He could then thank her for letting him see the puppet show. Perhaps he could even walk on the land to take it to her house.

Mother's words interrupted Wong Ting's thoughts. She was still explaining. "Yes, my husband. There are three jade dragons on a fine silver bracelet. It also has three green emeralds and three red rubies along the edges."

Wong Ting thought the lost bracelet must belong to his Kind Lady. Hers had emeralds and rubies on the wide band of silver.

Father sounded eager, "And if we find it?"

"We will be rich, my husband. The reward was announced but an hour ago. They will pay three pieces of gold for its return."

Wong Ting smiled happily. Gold! Three pieces of gold! If they had three pieces of gold, all of his dreams for them would come true all at once.

As they fished, Father cautioned, "Be careful that we do not tangle our net with the nets of those who seek the dragons."

As they worked, Father spoke again as if thinking out loud. "If the Fortune of Heaven is with us this day, there will be gold in the money belt instead of coppers."

Mother chatted as she worked. She went on to tell more about what the women in the next sampan knew regarding this exciting happening. "The three dragons have been in the rich merchant's family for two hundred years."

Two hundred years! That was a long, long time. No wonder they offered a reward of three pieces of gold. His Kind Lady must indeed be unhappy to have lost it.

Although he had seen it closely only once, Wong Ting remembered how the bracelet shone in the sunlight. But it had not been the three green emeralds or the three red rubies which had pleased him most. Best of all, he liked the small, fat jade dragons which had danced when his Kind Lady moved her arm.

"Listen," Mother was saying, "we *must* find the bracelet. If we had gold, we would not have to fish all day for something to eat. We would not lose part of each catch because of worn nets. There would be a larger sampan for us who are so crowded, and Lim Sang could have this one."

Each time they pulled up the net, the family crowded around to see if a shininess could be seen inside the webbing. But they found nothing but a few soggy twigs and some small stones.

They fished all the rest of that day and until the hour of full darkness closed in around them. Only then did Father give up. "Stretch the net," he ordered. "We go to drop anchor in the harbor."

The days went by too quickly. Only when the family was truly hungry did they pole upstream to fish for fish instead of for the three dragons.

Once Wong Ting saw the orange-colored sampan close enough to shout, "Do the dragons still sleep in the mud?"

Tsu Li had called back, "Yes, and is there one river family who does not dream of earning the pieces of gold?"

Two days later, just before third rice, the sun dipped lower and lower in the west. It was then that a spot of color caught Wong Ting's eye. Red! Far upstream skimmed a boat with something red painted on its prow.

Could it be the pirates? Wong Ting watched anxiously, but the boat was still too far away to see clearly.

As it moved closer, Wong Ting stiffened. He counted six oars. Six! Had not Tsu Li's father said the river pirates had a red devil fish painted on their prow? Had not he said they came in a boat with six swift oars?

"Pirates!" Wong Ting yelled from the stern.

At this same moment, other sampan families must have seen the robbers, too. They began pulling up their nets. Soon they began poling downstream as fast as they could go, the Winds of Heaven billowing their sails.

Without being told, everyone pulled eagerly on the net. Then everyone, even Mother, grabbed poles and began pushing hard to get away from the river pirates.

One by one the other boats skimmed quickly past them,

leaving them far behind. Soon there were no more sampans between them and the robbers.

"Hurry," Wong Ting urged. "Hurry, my father. The pirates are right behind us."

But something was wrong. Wong Ting glanced back to watch Father's pole. It did not have the strength it once had before the fever came to weaken him.

Working even faster, Wong Ting dug in his pole, leaning harder each time to shove them faster across the Wu. He wanted to make up for the slowness of Father's poling.

Several large junks lay in mid-river. They did not raise their sails to flee from the brigands. Their decks were high above the river. A swinging club could easily knock a robber from the climbing ropes.

But not so with sampan families. Four or five pirates, waving sharp, curved knives, could easily force a river father to hand over his money belt. As the Old One once said, "It is just plain foolishness to try to fight back when there is one against many."

Wong Ting did not want Father to have to face these cruel brigands. Wong Ting did not want Father to untie the money belt and hand it over to these pirates.

As Wong Ting bent to the pole, each minute seemed to last forever. To Wong Ting, the sampan seemed almost to stand still upon the water. But it did not. Farm lands slid by rapidly. In fact, soon they should be seeing the tall buildings of the City of Min.

The tide speeded them on their way downstream, and the Winds of Heaven, blowing toward the South China Sea, filled their sail. Still they did not lose sight of the river pirates. The six oars kept moving rapidly, gradually closing the space between the two boats.

Wong Ting had worked so fast he was now gasping for breath. He glanced back to see how near the brigands were.

The red devil fish was so close now that its long, twisting arms seemed ready to pounce on them.

Father asked, "Do they slow their swiftness, Wong Ting?"

"No! They move with the speed of a water snake," he answered, his heart pounding with fear.

Father yelled toward the stern where the Old One sat. "Steer for the north canal. We will try to escape behind the Water Gate."

Hope crept into Wong Ting's heart at these words. Father would outsmart the robbers. Father would save them from the river pirates.

Between strokes of his pole, Wong Ting watched the western horizon. He was glad to see it shining pinkly with the glow of the approaching sunset. If they hurried, they might reach the Water Gate before it closed down for the night.

Lim Sang, Wong Ting, and Father worked faster and faster, hope of saving themselves adding speed to their movements.

It was a good plan, Wong Ting thought, to try for the Water Gate. With the robbers so close, Father must have known that they might not reach the harbor in time.

Wong Ting felt the deck twist suddenly from under his feet. He was thrown to the deck and crashed up against the gunwale. Sheepishly, he scrambled to his feet. He should have realized Grandfather would wait until the last possible second to swing the bow around, into the mouth of the canal. Not expecting this trick from their intended victims, the river pirates had swept on past the small opening too quickly to turn and follow.

Wong Ting immediately eased up on his poling, smiling at the Old One's cleverness. But Father chided him. "Do not rest your pole," he said. "The robbers may still catch us. I may still have to put our money belt into their greedy hands."

At this wise advice, Wong Ting began to push with all of his strength. In a few moments he turned to look back past the stern. The devil boat had entered the canal. Father had been right. Somehow the robbers had managed to turn around. The six oars were splashing rapidly.

"The pirates!" Wong Ting shouted, bending to the pole. He sighed with relief to see the outline of the arched bridge just ahead. Soon they would skim under the Water Gate.

Afraid the gate man would drop it before they could find safety beyond the bridge, Wong Ting yelled, "He la, ho la! Hold the gate! Hold the gate!"

Lim Sang also called out in a loud, anxious voice. "Pirates! Pirates! Save us!"

Would the gate man hear their cries?

A few hard shoves with the poles sent the sampan skimming under the arch like a frightened bird. Almost at once Wong Ting heard a loud, creaking sound. The heavy Water Gate crashed downward. They were safe. Now the brigands could not steal the money belt.

Just before the heavy gate splashed into place, Wong Ting caught a glimpse of the devil boat. The river pirates were leaning on their oars as if too tired to move now that the chase was useless.

Wong Ting, Lim Sang, and Father called up their grateful thanks to the gate man on top of the arched bridge. He waved at them and grinned a toothless smile, seeming pleased at his part in their rescue.

They dropped anchor just beyond the closed Water Gate. Lim Sang and Father sat near the cabin door talking over their narrow escape. Tired from the hard work, Wong Ting leaned against the gunwale listening to them.

Mother said, "What this family needs now is something hot to eat. And then to bed. Watch the children, Wong Ting. I go to cook third rice."

Chapter 9:
The Big Fish

Not until the Moon of Hungry Ghosts came to the river Wu did Father finally decide to go down to the South China Sea to fish. All through the Lotus Moon the clouds had been too heavy, the winds too strong. It was not at all like the summer weather they usually enjoyed.

Some mornings, to Wong Ting's delight, Father ordered their sampan steered to the place near where the Kind Lady had lost her bracelet. How excited they were as they fished for the jade dragons! High hopes filled their hearts and showed on their smiling faces.

Often they heard the jeering of some river people. "What a foolish waste of good fishing hours," one man shouted, shaking his head as if not understanding such lack of judgment.

Father did not get angry. He always smiled and answered good-naturedly, "The dragons still sleep in the mud."

Back would come the answer, "What you say is true, but the bracelet has burrowed too deep to be caught by our clumsy nets," and laughing at Father, the man would pole past them on his way to the fishing grounds.

Whenever they fished near the dragons' hiding place, they would drag the net through the Wu many times before giving up. As it was pulled out of the river, they would all stare inside, hoping to see a shininess that would be the wide silver bracelet. But so far they had not been successful.

Father, trying to cheer them up, would say, "The dragons escape us this morning, but some happy day we will pull them from their home in the mud. Some day we will earn those pieces of gold."

With all of his heart, Wong Ting hoped Father was right.

One rosy dawn, as Wong Ting looked for his skull cap, Father said, "After our stomachs are satisfied, we will go downstream. If the Fortune of Heaven smiles on us, we may catch a sailfish in the ocean."

It had been more than twelve moons since they had tried fishing in the deep waters of the South China Sea. Only during this particular season could sampans venture out on the ocean. Only during the hot months of the year were the waves calm enough for such small boats.

Wong Ting's heart beat a happy rhythm of gladness. He was so anxious to get started, he gulped down his rice without chewing it. Perhaps this very day their net would bring up a big fish. If that happened, the money belt would sag with heaviness, and his dreams would no longer be just dreams.

With the morning land breeze filling their sail and everyone helping with the poles, they soon came to the City of Wang at the mouth of the river Wu.

As they crossed the bay, Father cautioned, "Watch your steering, Wong Ting. Head straight into the swells."

Gripping the oar more tightly, Wong Ting nodded. "I'll be careful. Very careful."

Looking ahead at the billowing straw-matting sail, Wong Ting felt grateful for its help. Without a sail, no sampan would dare to venture out on the ocean. Poles were as useless as twigs in the South China Sea.

Just as in the monsoon, Wong Ting felt the sampan being picked up high, then dropped down again by the waves made by the meeting of the river Wu with the ocean. It was exciting, and a little frightening, too.

After they passed the swells, everyone dropped his pole, shoving it up against the gunwale out of the way. Here the ocean was so deep that poles could not touch the bottom.

Stepping quickly to the stern, Father took the steering oar and scuttled quickly between the many sampans and junks which were already busy with their nets.

When they reached a clear space, Father seemed satisfied. "We'll fish here," he said, motioning to the Old One to steer.

Hopes high, the family hurried to pull down the heavy pile of webbing. Lim Sang and Father shoved back the two front sections of the cabin roof to give more room on the deck. Excited, eager hands lowered the net.

Without being reminded, Wong Ting immediately busied himself with the dip net. Leaning against the gunwale, he checked the worn places. As he retied the frayed knots, he wished again that they could have a newer, stronger net. This one was worn out. He worried because it might not hold against the great weight of a flatfish.

The steady rhythm of the flapping sail was soothing to Wong Ting's ears. He began to daydream. While he worked, Wong Ting looked longingly across the bay to the City of Wang. He could see the street near the busy wharf swarming with people and wondered if he would ever have a chance to feel the land under his feet.

Wong Ting's brow puckered with the same nagging doubts. Should he forget his secret wish? Was it just plain madness, as Tsu Li said? No! Wong Ting could not believe that. He would never believe that.

As his fingers skillfully mended the dip net, Wong Ting kept wishing that there was some way for a river boy to earn money. If he had as many coppers as he had fingers and toes, he would buy the things his family needed.

First of all, he would get a new, strong fishing net. Theirs had to be mended each time it was used. After it was hung on the poles to dry, everyone helped to find the weak places. Even with many willing hands to do this, it always took a long time.

It fell to Wong Ting to take care of the smaller net by himself. Because full darkness usually came before this could be done, Wong Ting finished the task every morning just after first rice, unless Father needed him to pole or steer.

When the sun was directly overhead, the men were called in for second rice. Later, Wong Ting sat in front of his food without a tug of hunger. He felt discouraged. So far they had only a few Japanese catfish. These could have been caught up at the fishing grounds without bothering to make the long journey to the South China Sea.

Unless they managed to get a big fish this day, his dreams for them all would be just dreams. Nothing more.

No sooner had Wong Ting returned to the deck than Father shouted, "Up with the net."

Hopefully, Wong Ting waited close by, holding the dip net by its long handle. As soon as the webbing was drawn up into a purse-like pocket, he began to scrape its sides carefully, anxious to scoop up all the fish into the smaller hand net.

As the dip net turned to come out, the water began to churn wildly. Wong Ting's heart jumped with happiness. Something was splashing around inside the net like a big fish. It felt heavy as a big fish. As he raised the dip net, he could see a pointed nose and a row of sharp teeth. The wide, flat tail slapped the top of the ocean, dashing cold sea water all over Wong Ting, but he scarcely noticed it, so intent was he on his job.

Lim Sang shouted joyfully, "The Fortune of Heaven is with us this day. It is a sailfish. I have seen bigger ones, but this is a good size."

As he spoke, he continued to hold his end of the heavy net high to close in the pocket. Then the fish could not leap out.

Father urged, "Hurry, Wong Ting, my arms ache with the great weight of this fish."

Wong Ting tightened his hold on the bamboo handle. He pulled and pulled. With all of his strength, he lifted the dip net higher and higher. He had never before felt a fish that was as heavy as this one.

As Wong Ting struggled with the heaviness, beads of perspiration stood out on his forehead and slid down his cheeks. Up, up moved Wong Ting's arms, his muscles bulging under the great weight of this big fish.

With a mighty effort, Wong Ting finally cleared the gunwale. Then, suddenly, the dip net went limp. The sailfish had fallen through a hole in the worn-out netting. With a big splash, the fish flopped back into the sea.

Wong Ting stood where he was without moving. Dazed, he stared glumly at the ever widening circles on top of the water where the sailfish had disappeared.

He kept asking himself what he had done wrong. He felt somehow that it was his fault.

Lim Sang threw an arm about Wong Ting's shoulders. "We'll catch another big fish, perhaps next summer," Lim Sang said.

"Next summer?" Wong Ting groaned.

"Yes, my son," Father offered, holding the frayed netting between his fingers. "Now that the dip net is no longer whole, we can fish no more this day."

Wong Ting blinked his eyes to keep tears from forming. He did not want the others to see them.

Gently Father explained, "Look here, my son. It was not carelessness that lost us the fish. It was the weakness of this old dip net. The webbing was too worn to hold against the great weight of that fish. It has been worrying me for some time. I thought something like this might happen. I kept hoping the money belt could buy a new one this season, but that was not possible. That was the main reason we did not come down to the ocean earlier in the summer. That and the bad weather."

In spite of this lengthy explanation, Wong Ting had never been so disappointed in all of his twelve years of growing up. Gloomily, he helped to pull in the big net and stretch it over the three poles for drying.

When Father said, "Good! The wind is changing. The breeze will speed our long journey north," Wong Ting picked up his pole and moved slowly toward the stern.

All the way up the river, Wong Ting scarcely knew what he was doing. His heart was heavy. He kept thinking about the lost fish.

It was all very well for Father to blame the weakness of the dip net. But, perhaps if Wong Ting had only worked more quickly...

Wong Ting listened to the steady lifting and pushing of his pole. Up and down. Up and down. It kept saying to him over and over again, "You failed! You failed! You failed!"

Chapter 10:
The Jade Dragons Again

Wong Ting's disappointment over losing the big fish did not lessen with the passing days. But, as Lim Sang said, perhaps when the Lotus Moon came again next summer, or the Moon of Hungry Ghosts, the weather would be right for a trip to the ocean. Maybe then he would have another chance to pull up a sailfish. Had not Father promised to buy a new dip net before they fished again in the South China Sea?

After the loss of the big fish, the Old One sat on a stool near the cabin door, patiently mending the small hand net. It was such a tedious chore that it had taken two full fishing days.

While he worked, the family gathered baskets full of water chestnuts. These brown nuts grew under the surface of the water where the river was shallow. Although they did not bring in as many coppers as fish did, this task kept idle hands busy and helped to push worrying thoughts away.

After the dip net was rewoven, Father often spent some hours of each morning fishing near the place on the Wu where the Kind Lady had lost her bracelet. Eager hands cheerfully lifted the heavy net, hope of earning the gold pieces still alive in all of their hearts.

But they were not successful. Neither were other river families. Whenever they passed each other on the Wu, the greeting was no longer, "Good day and good fishing," but, "Do the dragons still sleep in the mud?"

One morning, not long after their return to the City of Min from the South China Sea, the dawn light was beginning to brighten the ceiling of the sleeping cabin. Wong Ting lay on his straw matting with closed eyes, but he was wide awake. He was busy with his thoughts, trying to think of some way his family could find the jeweled bracelet.

Wong Ting sighed. If he pulled the jade dragons from the mud, all of his dreams would come true, and all at once. The three pieces of gold would buy everything the family needed and many other things beside.

As he thought about the lost bracelet, a frown changed to a smile. Wong Ting sat up on his sleeping mat. A plan had just popped into his head. It seemed like a good plan. He would fish for the dragons, but not with their larger net. That one would be too heavy for him to handle by himself. He would use the long handled dip net. Where they had anchored last night the river was quite shallow. Besides, it was just below the place in the Wu where the Kind Lady had lost her bracelet.

The more he thought about it, the more Wong Ting liked his plan. Quietly squeezing past the bamboo curtain, he stepped out on the deck, shivering in the chilly dampness of the dawn.

Groping in the dimness for the dip net, which was always stored on top of the cabin roof, Wong Ting lifted it down. He was careful not to make any noise. He did not want anyone to know about his plan until he pulled the jade dragons from their home in the mud. Besides, he knew Father and Mother, Lim Sang, and the Old One needed their rest. They were always so tired. Only a full night's sleep could give them back the strength used up in the work of each day.

Rolling up the long sleeves on his padded coat, Wong Ting leaned far out over the gunwale, close to the bow. Holding tightly to the long handle, he lowered the net until he felt one edge touching the bottom of the Wu. Walking back along the deck toward the stern, he felt the bamboo circle scraping against the mud.

Hopefully, Wong Ting lifted up the net. He rested it a moment on the bow to drain off the water. In it there was only a handful of soggy leaves, a few twigs, and stones.

Somewhat discouraged, Wong Ting went on fishing for the dragons until he heard the family stirring around inside the cabin. Quickly, he returned the dip net to its place on top of the curved roof and went inside. No one seemed to realize that he had been up long before anyone else. At least no one mentioned it. Wong Ting was glad he did not have to answer any questions. He wanted to keep his plan to himself. He wanted to find the bracelet by himself.

Whenever they anchored close to the place where the jewelry had been lost, Wong Ting awoke before the dawn and continued his search. Each time, as he scraped the dip net against the bottom of the Wu, he dreamed of earning the gold for his family.

One morning, just as the first streaks of sunlight tinged the eastern sky, Wong Ting looked into his net. He caught his breath. Something sparkled inside the webbing.

Before picking it up, he called out in a loud, proud voice, "The bracelet! The bracelet! Mother! Father! Lim Sang! I found the bracelet!"

The family stumbled through the door, rubbing sleep-filled eyes. They shoved against Wong Ting in their eagerness to see the dip net. They stood close by as Wong Ting dumped it out on the mat-covered deck. Something shiny did fall out. Wong Ting's fingers trembled as he picked it up. After rubbing it against his trousers to wipe off the mud, bitter disappointment filled his heart. He ducked his head so that the others would not see his sudden tears.

Everyone laughed, all except Wong Ting.

Lim Sang reached over and took it from Wong Ting. Lim Sang teased, "It is not even a one dragon bracelet. Like the poor madman, my brother does not know a piece of broken anchor when he sees it," and Lim Sang turned away with an amused smile on his lips. With a quick movement, he tossed the shiny metal back into the Wu and went inside the cabin.

Discouraged by his failure, Wong Ting followed him.

Father said, "It is a little early, but since we are up, we will get a good start to this day."

Wong Ting ate first rice without tasting the hot food. Of one thing he was sure. He would keep right on trying to find the dragons, no matter how much Lim Sang might tease him.

Most everyone else had gone back to fishing for fish instead of for the bracelet. Whenever Wong Ting heard the question, "Do the three dragons still sleep in the mud?" he felt hope rise within him at Father's reply. "Yes, and we are the one river family who still seeks the slumbering dragons."

No taunts discouraged Father, and neither was Wong Ting ready to give up the search. Every chance he had, he fished for the silver bracelet.

Early one morning Wong Ting again lowered the dip net while the family still slept. The first two times that he emptied out the net onto the matting, he saw nothing but a tangle of twigs and roots.

Now he again brought up the hand net. He blinked rapidly, thinking he still dreamed. A bright something lay partly hidden inside the webbing.

Wong Ting did not shout for his family. He reached in and picked up the Kind Lady's bracelet. Even with the thick coating of river mud on it, he could see the three red rubies and the three green emeralds. As he looked at the little jade dragons, his heart overflowed with his happiness.

Wong Ting had found the bracelet!

How pleased his Kind Lady would be to have it returned to her! It was almost too good to be true, but it was true. Here in his hands, Wong Ting held the beautiful jewelry. He had pulled the dragons from their home in the mud.

Wong Ting wiped the bracelet across his padded trousers to remove the dirt. Then he stood there on the deck, rubbing a finger across the smoothness of the bright silver. Shaking it gently, he watched, fascinated, as the three jade dragons danced.

But he was being selfish. The family would want to know, too, about this blessing that had come to them.

Wong Ting squeezed past the bamboo curtain and stepped into the cabin. He looked from mat to mat. They still slept, but he must awaken them. Nothing as exciting as this had ever happened to them.

"Wake up, Father! Mother! Lim Sang! Grandfather!" Wong Ting called out in a loud, happy voice.

They sat up one by one, looking at him sleepily.

"I found the dragons," Wong Ting explained, holding the beautiful bracelet out for them to see.

At first no one said a word, but their faces showed that they thought they were still dreaming. For a breathless moment, they just stared.

Suddenly Lim Sang jumped to his feet, as if realizing what this would mean to him. He hugged Wong Ting until his breath left him. Talking very fast, Lim Sang shouted, "Look what my brother found. It *is* the three dragon bracelet this time."

Father and Mother began asking questions that Wong Ting answered as quickly as he could. The Old One's toothless smile showed his pleasure in this good happening.

Father finally reached his arm out. Taking the bracelet in trembling fingers, he said, "It is for this son to say how the gold will be spent."

Speaking so fast his words tumbled out, Wong Ting listed

the things he would buy for them all, knowing the jade dragons would make all his dreams come true, these and many, many more.

When he paused for breath, Father nodded in approval. "That is all very well, my son," he agreed, "and very fine plans they are, too. But what of yourself? Surely, you have one dream of your very own?"

Smiling happily, Wong Ting answered, "Yes, Father. With your permission, I will take the jade dragons to my Kind Lady and thank her for the puppet show, and ..." He hesitated, hoping they would all understand about his secret wish. Then boldly he went on, "And, I *will walk on the land!*"

More Books from The Good and the Beautiful Library

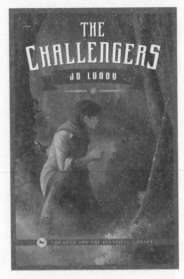

The Challengers
by Jo Lundy

Slave Boy in Judea
by Josephine Sanger Lau

The Three Gold Doubloons
by Edith Thacher Hurd

Tiger on the Mountain
by Shirley L. Arora